THE NABOB'S DESIGNING DAUGHTER

BOOK FOUR, THE UPSTART CHRISTMAS BRIDES

ALINA K. FIELD

HAVENLOCK PRESS

The Nabob's Designing Daughter
© 2022 Mary J. Kozlowski

ISBN 978-1-944063-42-9

Havenlock Press

PO Box 1891

La Mirada, CA 90637

December 20, 2022

Cover design by Dar Albert of Wicked Smart Designs

THE NABOB'S DESIGNING DAUGHTER

A wealthy nabob's daughter has designs on a handsome young doctor, but not the romantic sort, despite the one kiss he stole from her ages ago. The poor crofters she's been tending behind her father's back need more than a rich miss's potions; they need a real doctor. And fortunately, she has the leverage to provide one.

Ripped from his prestigious London practice to deliver a Highland duke's heir, a young doctor finds there are more snares awaiting him than a risky birth, including a surprise—and worthless—bequest. There's also his best friend's cousin, who's blossomed from mousey to heart-stirringly beautiful, with enough wiles to convince an ambitious man that his heart belongs in the Highlands

AN UNEXPECTED KISS

LATE SUMMER, 1820

EDINBURGH, SCOTLAND

*E*rrol Robillard leaned on the bar of the busy taproom of the inn that had once been his father's.

"Money, ye say?" Pherson MacIver tapped the top of the rough-hewn counter.

He ought to have known better than to ask the old skinflint for help. MacIver had bought the struggling business after Errol's father's death and built it up into one of the most prosperous posting inns in Edinburgh. He had plenty of money but lacked the generous heart that had caused Errol's father to struggle.

But, needs must. "Aye. With Beecham's death, I'm looking for help with the university fees. Two more years to go and I'll be a qualified physician and surgeon, and be able to pay you back."

The fat fellow grunted. "I'd heard aught was wrong there. Ship lost, they say." He mashed his rubbery lips together. "Here, now. If ye've need of work, why, I could use a man like you. Pay a salary. Save up if ye like and go back to that college."

The ale suddenly tasted sour. He would not turn aside from his ambitions despite—or perhaps because of—his lowly roots. "I thank ye for the offer." His mam had taught him manners. His da had taught him to not burn his boats. But more than anything, he wanted to turn the rest of his tankard over MacIver's head. "I'll be off," he said. "Early day tomorrow."

"Beecham's funeral. Grand affair it will be."

"Aye."

He took himself off to the single room he rented near the University.

The weather the next morning had been as weepy as the mourners inside the respectable townhouse that was the home of the late Horace Beecham.

The funeral reception had ended; friends and business associates had left the widow and her large brood to their private grief. They'd all departed, except for himself, Errol Robillard, but then he was more than a friend or business associate. At Beecham's behest and expense, Errol had attended a day school with the man's two eldest boys, William and Peter, and, when not studying or laboring at his father's inn, he'd worked hard at Beecham's textile warehouse.

William Beecham was his best friend. Whether he was a good enough friend to continue paying Errol's schooling was a question he hadn't yet raised, and his university fees were due.

He needed to speak to William, later, when Mrs. Beecham and the rest of the family had retired. But first, a breath of air, damp though it might be, was in order, before he made his vulgar but necessary inquiry.

In the garden, the herb-scented air filled his lungs but didn't clear his head or comfort his heart. Beecham's death followed too closely on his own father's passing two years earlier. In fact, he still grieved his mother's passing several years before that.

A rain-slicked flagstone path snaked through well-tended beds of herbs, vegetables, and flowers to the shed at the back, partially concealed by an overgrown elm tree. He moved toward a sheltered bench on the small patch of grass, passing the raised beds filled with vegetables and the medicinal plants the Beechams' eccentric cousin, Ann Strachney, raised for her concoctions of tisanes and teas.

A plop of water landed upon his nose, and the heavens suddenly reopened with gusto. Before he could retreat inside a sudden cry from the vicinity of a tall elm had him rushing there.

A ladder teetered, a half-booted foot searching for purchase under a black skirt.

"Stay still." He reached, but the ladder teetered again, and an armful of skirts plopped onto him, knocking him flat on his back, almost knocking the wind from him.

A grubby hand pushed back a wet tangle of light brown hair. Ann Strachney's eyes widened, her already pink cheeks darkened, and her lips—just as pink, surprisingly lush—formed a perfect O.

Gad, she was lovely. An oval face, porcelain skin, and eyes the color of a stormy sea. How had he not noticed? Another lock of hair fell, she wriggled, and his male parts stirred. He clamped a hand on her to get her to stop.

"Oh," she said, getting the word out. "I'm so sorry. I was…" She waved a hand. "The tree branch. The green house…"

He lifted his head and stopped her chatter, his lips soft against her own.

The wind gusted and glass exploded. He yanked her head down and cradled it in his hand and inhaled the scents of flowers and springtime, honey and bees. The hot breaths on his neck, the press of her breasts against his chest roused him more.

She mumbled, tickling him.

"What did you say?" he asked. "Are you alright?"

A BATTLE RAGED WITHIN ANN STRACHNEY, OR A strange, unfamiliar mêlée of nerves and blood, tingles and shivers, and a hot pooling of… what was this? She was stretched atop a muscled chest, her nose buried against hot flesh that smelled of starch and shaving soap, and a large weight pressed against her back. A tree branch or… oh. It was a hand and it had started to move, and she didn't want it to stop. Steam ought to be rising from her wet hair and gown. She ought to be melting.

Errol was holding her. Errol Robillard, the handsome, teasing boy who'd grown into a braw charming man. He was stroking her back. And a minute before he'd looked into her eyes and… what she saw there she didn't recognize.

But she liked how it felt. She didn't want it to stop.

"Are you injured?" he asked, sounding more himself.

Was she? How could she possibly tell when she was lying atop a gentleman…

"No," she said, pushing herself up on her forearms. Errol grinned up at her, eyelids drooping wolfishly over eyes that had gone impossibly black. He'd lost his hat, and his tawny curls stuck out like the start of a lion's mane.

Heat flooded her cheeks yet again. He was, as usual, impossibly handsome, but this was something more.

"I beg your pardon. But thank you for… for breaking my fall. Are *you* injured?"

He raised up on his elbows. "How could I be injured by you falling on me, Mouse?"

"Right." The hated nickname. It was clear he'd lost his mind for a moment and he regretted that kiss. Even if she was one to brew love potions—and she wasn't—he'd never think of her as a desirable woman.

"By all that's holy, what are the two of ye doin'?"

Her cousin, Edme Beecham, her dearest friend in all the world, stood there, mouth open in shock.

Ann fumbled to her knees. "It's not—"

"And on the day of da's funeral." She reached for Ann and helped her up, her mouth grim, but her eyes beginning to twinkle.

"Ann fell off the ladder," Errol said. "She was… what the devil *were* you doing up there?"

They were back to normal. "There's no need for foul language. I was trying to cut the tree branch."

"The gardener could have—"

"William had to let him go." Ann shook out her sodden skirts. "Finances, he said."

Errol's face fell, and she remembered: Uncle was paying his university fees.

"*I* would have paid the gardener," she said. "I do have *some* money." More than some. Her godmother had died only a few weeks ago—another sorry loss—leaving her a tidy inheritance, one that the rest of the family knew nothing about. And she intended to keep it that way for now.

She was of age. She loved her aunt and her cousins, but it didn't seem that her father would ever return from India. Mayhap it was time for her to travel there and meet the man who'd left when she was no more than a wee thing.

She could even have paid the gardener his pittance out of the pin money she'd saved. He only worked part time. She'd done much of the planting and pruning and plucking here.

The boys might call her mouse, but she was strong. She carried buckets, and beat rugs, and climbed ladders to clean windows and swat at flies. Her mother and aunt had been a farmer's daughters, and there was no slacking allowed in the household. Everyone pitched in, even the littlest Beechams when they were old enough. She'd even helped Aunt through childbirth with the last three of her babes, and nursed Uncle those last days of his illness. His death had come hard upon that of her mother and godmother. After the funeral reception, she'd had to escape to her plants.

The general grief and exhaustion had made her clumsy, and well, the axe had slipped from her fingers. Lucky that Errol hadn't passed below five minutes earlier. It might have dropped on his handsome, opinionated head.

Leaving him sputtering, she hurried into the small shed that she called her greenhouse. Broken pottery, dirt, and wee green stems with curly white roots lay strewn on the table under the broken window.

She swore under her breath. "My *nigella sativa* is done for."

"What was it for?" Errol asked.

"She's making a medicinal oil with it," Edme said.

Ann gently righted a clump with a seedling and set it into an intact pot. "The oil is said to be effective against infections of the lungs." She held her breath, waiting for him to laugh at her. When she looked, she found him examining the plants.

"*Nigella sativa*," he said. "I *have* heard of it."

"Here, Ann." A warm woolen shawl settled over her shoulders. "Please can you come back to the house? Mum is beside herself and I can't find your valerian root tea. She'll want it to sleep."

"Valerian root?" Errol said. "It's been known to cause heart palpitations. Perhaps some hot milk—"

"Thank you, Errol." Edme raised one strawberry blonde eyebrow at him.

"Heart problems?" Ann bit her lip. "*Culpeper's Guide* didn't mention heart problems. Do you have a reference?"

He was looking at her as if she'd sprouted two heads.

She lifted her chin. "If there's aught you know—new research, that is, perhaps when you visit William, you could tell me—"

"Not likely, Mouse. I mainly meet him at the warehouse or a pub."

Anger rose in her. "You blast…" She bit her lip again. She'd grown up with male cousins and knew all the words for cursing, but it didn't mean she had to stoop to use them on this arrogant numbskull. "You could… you could write to me about your pharmacopeia lectures and books. Edme, do you think Aunt will mind?"

"Why would she if you can cure her cough? Come on, the both of you, stop," she waved a hand, "whatever it is you're doing here, and come out of the rain. William is looking for you Errol. And Mum needs that tea."

Her aunt's needs must come first. She could start a new batch of plantings.

With a glance at the poor wee things, Ann wrapped her shawl tighter and let herself be led along by Edme. While she brewed tea for her aunt and helped her to bed, William would talk to Errol, and what would her cousin say? She'd heard some of the whispers about the money troubles. With her uncle dead, creditors were more careful about advancing capital to the son.

William was competent, though, and honest; he would find his way. She could offer to invest, but she doubted he'd accept financial help from a woman, and his cousin the mouse to boot. She'd wait and see before mentioning the subject.

Errol likely wouldn't want a woman's help either, but he must finish his education. If William couldn't help him, she'd find a way to do it herself.

A FEW DAYS LATER...

Ann lingered outside William's study, shamelessly eavesdropping on the masculine voices within.

"'Struth, I'm relieved, Errol. I could pony up some of your school fees, but not all, and not for all the terms you have left. Though mayhap if things turn around with the new shipment from Bruges—"

"Doona worry. This Henderson fellow assures me there are funds aplenty to finish my education. I'll call on him tomorrow to sign the agreement."

"And are you free of Da's year of servitude?"

Errol's agreement with Uncle had included a year of servitude? She pressed her ear to the door.

"He didn't mention one. Though I didn't begrudge your father that obligation. 'Twas the least I could do, spending a year tending to the warehouse folk and their families."

"And who is this generous benefactor?"

"I've no clue. He wishes to remain anonymous."

"Fancy that. Will you say goodbye to my mother before you leave? Have a look at her? Ann's been dosing her with a tonic that seems to be doing her good."

Errol's chuckle rumbled through the door. "Women's potions. Watch them though. Some of those plants can be dangerous in the wrong doses."

"Ah, yes. I hear you had words with Ann about her valerian tea." A chair creaked through a long pause. "That was after you were having warm words when Edme interrupted you. My cousin has grown up, hasn't she? You're a sly one, Errol."

Errol laughed, and it sounded false. "Me and the mouse? The silly lass fell off a ladder and I caught her, was all."

Mouse? Silly lass?

Ann bit her lip.

Silly, was she? And the big lout thought her *potions* were a joke. She ought to go back to Mr. Henderson's office and…

A year of servitude? Why hadn't she thought of that?

She squared her shoulders, rapped on the door, and pushed it open. Two sets of startled eyes turned her way and both men stood.

Oh heavens, the tingling and melting started again, and she steeled herself against the shivers. Errol was more handsome than ever today. Tall and broad in a well-cut coat of dark superfine—his benefactor,

Beecham was in the textile trade, after all—his curls had been tamed and his neckcloth sported an elegant knot. "Good day to you, Errol. William, Aunt says Errol must stop and say farewell. And this silly lass is wishing you my own farewell now, Errol."

He blinked and opened his mouth.

"Yes, I *was* eavesdropping outside," she said.

"Ann, I—"

She put up her hand. "No false apologies please."

His eyes narrowed on her and he finally sighed. "Well, I'll go now and see Mrs. Beecham. I need to be off soon."

Aunt would keep Errol talking for half an hour, giving her time to do what she must.

William came around his desk. "I'll come too."

"You both go ahead," she said. "I have an errand. Errol, I look forward to your letters."

William gave a startled laugh. Errol smiled, but his color rising told the true tale of his feelings, and likely his intention to forget she ever asked his help.

"You didn't tell William, did you? Errol promised to share knowledge with me from his pharmacopeia lectures. You won't mind, William, will you?"

She turned on her heel and left. Footsteps resounded behind her, both men following her.

"Ann," William called. "Perhaps Errol will be too busy to—"

"To write to your mousey cousin?"

"Here now, Ann—"

"No, William," Errol said. "We've been caught out. Ann, my sincere apologies. I meant you no harm."

That apology *did* sound sincere. "So, you will write?"

"You've shamed me into it."

Well, that was lowering.

"I've just opened a letter from your father, Ann," William said. "He's returning soon and wants you to live with him. You won't be here to receive letters from Errol."

She stopped in the corridor, her heart pounding. Blasted William was trying to save his friend from the onerous task of writing letters.

And as for going to live with her father? Curiosity mixed with dread. What would he be like? She had only the vaguest memory of him. He'd deposited his wife and child with the Beechams and set off for India to make his fortune. Letters came once a year; short, stiff letters penned by a secretary, her mother said, because Father's handwriting was atrocious. Still, her mother had missed him and longed for his return, and so had she.

"You may forward Errol's letters until I can let him know my direction."

"He may not think it proper."

"Don't be silly." Surely her father wouldn't mind her receiving letters about scientific matters. She shook off a spot of worry, fetched her bonnet and gloves and went out through the kitchens and down a side street where she couldn't be viewed from the parlor window. She hoped Mr. Henderson had time to see her. One condition must be added to that contract.

Mousey indeed.

AT CASTLE KINMARTY

DECEMBER 1822

THE SCOTTISH HIGHLANDS

"Three single noblemen, and no other young ladies." Benedict Strachney rubbed his plump, kid-leather encased palms together.

Respectably turned out by the valet he'd hired away from some English lord, his sober green frock coat, tailored for him in Edinburgh, topped a matching waist coat and buff breeches that did no honor to his form. Or rather his form spreading over the opposite bench did no honor to the fine craftsmanship of the garments.

"Yes, Father." Ann turned her gaze back to the coach window, lest he see the small smile she was fighting.

This December's weather had been mild, relatively speaking, the occasional snow melting under the regular rain showers. Outside, the weathered landscape rolled toward mist-covered hills and her insides tingled with anticipation. Upon his return, her father had traveled the length and breadth of Scotland and finally acquired Glenthistle.

Despite the lack of a bookstore, and well-stocked shops in the village of Kinmarty despite the lack of family, and despite that she had to pursue her interest in herbs and medicinals on the sly, she loved the Highlands, and she'd found friends here. She hated the poverty though, and did all she could, whenever she could, to alleviate it.

She pressed her gloved hand to the window and leaned forward to count the few sheep in the field and wave to the child tending them. The boy, Rolly Gillespie, had survived a bad fever the spring before, and it cheered her to see him so well.

Father angled his head to peer out and grunted.

She held her breath for a reprimand: *One did not need to acknowledge a crofter's child*. As if father had not once been one of those himself.

"That's Darleton's land," Father said. "I've a notion to offer to buy the title if they ever find the heir."

The last Baron Darleton had died only months before.

"I'll tear down that crumbling Mounth Tower and send the crofters packing. Put all the land to sheep. Might build a fishing lodge, though. Best angling in the

Highlands there, and 'twill all be mine." His gaze pinned her. "Now that's something to offer in the marriage settlements. Noblemen like their sport."

She bit her lip and turned her gaze back to the window. Perhaps if Darleton had opened his land to rich English anglers, his people wouldn't have suffered so much. He'd been a crotchety old recluse, or so everyone said. She'd called on him after seeing to the sick child, and he'd had his servant refuse to admit her. 'Twas shameful, his lack of care for his people, and they all hoped for better from the heir, whomever that might be.

But her father as Darleton? She'd learned soon enough that he could be heartless and cruel, an absolute bully when his will was openly challenged. She'd thought his sole focus was on having his daughter marry well, but buying the Darleton barony?

Perhaps she could find a way to squash his ambition there. "Mayhap the heir will be a single young man of good fortune looking for a wife," she said. *One who might be persuaded to do right by his tenants.*

Father grunted. "He'll need every penny of that good fortune. No, daughter, we must look higher to the noblemen at hand. Now, you will avoid the influence of Mrs. MacDonal, should she return from Edinburgh, which I've heard is in doubt, especially with the weather likely to turn foul." He paused and pressed his lips together. "Far better to attach yourself to the duchess during our stay."

She bit back a smile and smoothed the blue wool of

her cloak. Father's regard for the duchess was only higher by comparison to the lady's cousin, Mrs. MacDonal.

"Given that the duchess will soon be entering her confinement," she said, struggling to keep her tone earnest, "ought we not to have asked my aunt from Edinburgh along as chaperone? I'm sure the duchess would welcome her."

A low grumble rolled from the opposite bench. "Miss Livingston ought to have accompanied us."

Miss Livingston was the well-bred but impoverished English woman her father had hired to transform his daughter into a proper lady. A thin mournful spinster approaching her fortieth year, granddaughter of an earl, the lady had only succumbed to her current role when her last supporting relative passed away and she needed a home. Ann saw her misery but had not been able to draw her out.

"A merchant's widow is not high enough for this crowd. No, daughter. Should any man importune you, only make sure it is one of the single men of high station and we shall have you wed by Hogmanay."

Her father had established himself as a distinguished member of the local gentry and a justice of the peace, a huge social leap for a poor crofter's son.

Now, he aimed to move higher. Last year he'd had hopes of making Ann a duchess. *That* hadn't worked out, but her father hadn't given up hope of a title for his only child.

She swallowed a bubble of defiance that threatened

to spill over into a chuckle. It wouldn't do to appear amused. Given all the rows they'd had on the subject, any display of humor on her part would raise his suspicions.

He didn't need to know she wouldn't be the only single young lady attending this December house party of their near neighbors, the Duke and Duchess of Kinmarty. He didn't need to know that Mrs. MacDonal, the duchess's cousin, would most certainly be there as well. The lady had traveled to and from India—no mere Highland winter would keep her away. Even now, she might be on the road behind them, bringing along Ann's cousin, Edme.

As for his goal that she be wedded by Hogmanay... A pox on titles and high station; a reasonably handsome man who shared her interests would do, and he must respect her, and how wonderful it would be to be loved.

Ann turned back to the window, remembering that day in the garden with Errol. Despite the flash of raw interest she'd seen in his eyes, and heavens, the kiss, she knew he'd never court her. He didn't respect her, he'd never love her, and when he learned the truth, he might just roar at her worse than Father did when she challenged him.

Mr. Henderson might have already told Errol the *what*, but he'd promised to let her be the one to tell him the *who*.

If the mouse could but summon some bravery to tell him.

· · ·

DR. ERROL ROBILLARD PEERED OUT THE WINDOW OF Mrs. Penelope MacDonal's well-appointed carriage, paying scant heed to the conversation of his companions, especially the excited chatter of Edme Beecham.

This first venture north to the Highlands was proving to be as tiring as his recent travels to and from London, and the whole bloody matter was making him feel low.

Not that he would let anyone know. He had a reputation for smooth bonhomie to maintain. And, in fact, it was seldom that his spirits felt battered. He knew himself and his abilities, had always found the seed of opportunity in every situation, and had experienced only a few occasions when his sense of—well, confidence—had been shaken. Like the deaths of his parents and his benefactor. Or this unexpected yank to the outer reaches of nowhere, away from his destiny—a prestigious and prosperous London practice where he could pursue his goal of making money while doing good.

But it was temporary, not the death of his dreams at all, but in fact an enhancement, providing all went well. And it must. He wasn't inclined to be gloomy. Fate, and his hard-won medical skills, would carry him through.

Yet the distant hills sparkling with patches of melting snow, the long stretches of scrubby land, and the crackling brooks they passed did little to cheer him. Leaving the close-packed, unsanitary congestion of London and his home, Edinburgh for a place of wider spaces might raise another man's spirits. But he knew he'd find poverty, poorer hygiene, and earlier winter here. Famine, fevers and influenzas were regular visitors to the Highlands as well. One didn't have to be a graduate of the University of Edinburgh Medical School to know that. His mother's untimely death had proved it.

The coach rattled, pitching them sideways through a turn. Edme squeaked and grabbed the hand strap.

A goodhearted lass, but the silliest of the Beecham children, Edme had grown into a pert young lady with sparkling amber eyes and fiery hair much like his own late mother's. He might have flirted with her himself, except that she—and more importantly her brother William—were like family to him, and Errol valued his life. Though initially reluctant to put her into the care of Mrs. MacDonal, William had given in. This trip to the Highlands would remove her from the temptations of one of his new clerks. She'd have the fun of a Yuletide house party, and then perhaps a chance for an even longer stay with Edme's cousin, Ann Strachney.

He shifted in his seat. No one had said whether Ann would be at Castle Kinmarty, and he wasn't quite sure that he wanted to see her. He'd thought far too much about her since that last awkward parting. She'd called him out on his rudeness, and he'd deserved it.

"Almost there." Edme's seatmate, Mrs. MacDonal, sent Errol a blue-eyed wink that made him start.

Women flirted with him, had done so since his voice started changing. But he shook off the possibility that Mrs. MacDonal was doing so. After all, this attractive wealthy widow and cousin to the Duchess of Kinmarty had been both friendly and commanding at their first meeting when she appeared for tea with Mrs. Beecham, and again later when he visited her to consult about travel arrangements at the inn where she was staying. His instincts about women, honed by his youth in his father's coaching inn, were seldom wrong. She had no carnal interest in him.

Besides, her Indian manservant, a strapping, silent, beturbaned man who served as footman, groom, and majordomo, had hovered nearby during those discussions, allaying any hint of impropriety. At least any impropriety involving Errol.

Today, the man accompanied the coach astride a fine piece of horseflesh. Errol wished to blazes he was also riding alongside the coach on the other side, despite the frigid December weather.

"I, for one, will be glad to arrive," Mrs. MacDonal said. "Minny will have tea for us, and a glass of the Kinmarty whisky, if you're inclined to partake of something stronger."

Minny was Mrs. MacDonal's pet name for her cousin, the Duchess of Kinmarty.

"If she hasn't already gone into labor." She tightened the strings on her outlandishly large bonnet bedecked with feathers the same color as her startlingly blue eyes. "I'm so happy we shared a common destination, Doctor, and that we were able to convey you to Kinmarty more expeditiously and in greater comfort than the public coach."

"You haven't been very good company, Errol." Edme said.

The whole trip was upending his life. A house party? In December? In the Highlands? And a hostess ready to go into labor? It was madness.

Having just finished four grueling but invigorating years of study in Edinburgh, he'd been in London, preparing to leave his inn room for a meeting with the senior members of a practice he hoped to join. And then two letters had arrived, both forwarded from Edinburgh. One from a solicitor named Henderson, a man he'd met two years before, setting a meeting with him a few weeks hence at Castle Kinmarty to discuss two matters of business.

Castle Kinmarty was in the Highlands, and he had no plans to journey there. He would write Mr. Henderson and tell him to convey the information in a letter.

The haughty tone of the solicitor's letter had poked at his pride. He'd come from lowly roots, grandson of an Afro-Caribbean laborer who'd found his way to Edinburgh and son of an innkeeper and his Highlander wife. Both his parents had died too young, and Errol wouldn't have made his way this far without help, first from his father's friend, Eleazar Beecham, and then, upon Beecham's death, from a second benefactor.

Before his father's death, he'd dealt with inn visitors, worked in Beecham's business, and studied hard. When he'd mastered his Greek, and especially his Latin, he'd gone off to study chemistry—always useful when dealing with textiles—until one day he'd stumbled into Professor Monro's anatomy lecture.

Now he was a qualified physician and trained surgeon, from the premier school of medicine in all of Britain, perhaps all of the world.

Still fuming, he'd opened the second letter, this one from the Duke of Kinmarty, and it was a plum assignment indeed, lifting his mood. Summoned, he was, to deliver the duke's firstborn and heir—with luck the child would indeed be male, and of course healthy. Surely, the practice would welcome him back once the child was safely delivered. They could not turn down a physician summoned by a duke.

The coach came around a bend and the outline of a building loomed.

Edme gasped. "Is that it?"

"Indeed it is," Mrs. MacDonal said. "Castle Kinmarty. My husband and the duke spent many happy times here."

"It *is* old," Edme said. "Ann described it so, but I scarce believed her."

"Centuries old. And it's true, rather dilapidated in places, but we are making repairs."

Ann again. She'd asked him to write, and he had, and she hadn't replied to his letter.

The coach made a turn, and he ducked his head to peer out. Kinmarty was as magnificent as Edinburgh Castle. A central tower stood between wings lined with windows. Precious candlelight glimmered through them in the twilight. Kinmarty appeared to be a prosperous residence for the duke and his wife.

Quite remote though, and far from other medical resources. And in a building this old, sanitation would likely be suspect. Was the water sound? Home to tend to his sick grandmother and make peace with his wretched grandfather, his mother had succumbed to a fever contracted in a Highland castle not so very far from here.

"What of the more modern amenities?" he asked. "Fresh water and so forth?"

He wracked his brain trying to remember if there'd been any reports of fever in the Highlands this year. While making his clinical rounds, he'd attended more than one birth. Childbirth might be a risky business in the best of circumstances, much depending on the mother's health and anatomy. With luck, the duchess would be built for childbearing and the local midwife, if one should appear, would be competent and not an interfering fool.

As the carriage slowed, he shook off the worries and watched as Mrs. MacDonal's manservant leapt from his mount, handed over his reins, and nudged the duke's liveried footman out of the way. Mrs. MacDonal beamed at the dark-eyed man as he helped her out and escorted her to the door.

Edme's eyes went wide, her mouth dropped open, and she sent him a curious look. For all that she'd grown up with worldly brothers in a vibrant and cosmopolitan household, Edme could be an innocent goose.

Best not to observe the equally worldly Mrs.

Penelope MacDonal too closely. "Close your mouth, Edme." He climbed out and helped her down.

"Oh my," Edme breathed, looking around the overdone entry hall. "Oh my, Errol. Have you ever—" She leaned close and whispered. "If William and Peter and the little ones could see... oh, and the grounds. The hunting the duke has planned. They would be delirious with the chance to stalk a grand stag."

THEY HANDED OVER THEIR OUTER GARMENTS AND entered a grand room, the fireplace at one end almost the size of the bedchamber he'd shared with his father's man-of-all-work. Stag heads lined the walls, along with ancient weapons and tapestries. In the far corner, near the blazing fire, a woman rose from her chair, and hurried toward them, the man with her rising and following.

Attractive and dark-haired, she was heavy with child, but rosy-cheeked and smiling. Other than an awkward gait—to be expected—she moved swiftly and caught Mrs. MacDonal, in an embrace.

Introductions were made. Andrew MacDonal, Duke of Kinmarty was a well-formed man of about thirty, he would guess, his wife not quite that age, yet older than one might expect of a duke's wife bearing his first child. Most noblemen married young women, anxious for as many years as required to produce a male heir.

"So, you're the physician." The duke scanned him from head to toe and back up again. "You might wish to know that my lady—"

"No, Andrew." The duchess touched her husband's arm. "Dr. Robillard has only just arrived. There is no urgency. We must let him rest before we get down to business."

Her calm demeanor put him at ease. Demme, but he *was* nervous, and that wouldn't do. "Your grace, if it is your time, I am ready now."

The duke sent her a smug look. "You see, Fil. We men of action are always ready."

Minny or Fil. What was the duchess's Christian name?

The duke nodded to him, as if they were equals, and his confidence rose. "If there's something you wish to tell me about your condition, your grace," Errol said, "I'd most assuredly like to hear it."

"Are you having false labor, Minnie?" Mrs. MacDonal appeared beside him and handed him a glass of whisky. "The Kinmarty brew. Quite good, and it will settle your nerves for the night ahead, if it is indeed Minnie's time."

"Enough talk of my upcoming ordeal. Edme, Dr. Robillard, we welcome you to our Yuletide celebration. Andrew and I grew up in England and at least where Christmas is concerned, we've brought our English ways." She smiled. "Come the New Year, we'll celebrate Hogmanay the Scottish way. Now, you must refresh yourself, Doctor Robillard. Come closer to the fire." She nudged her cousin aside and led Errol to the hearth, whispering. "My husband is apprehensive."

"And you, Duchess?"

"No." She shivered. "Or, yes, in fact. My first, and at the advanced age of eight and twenty."

Nerves were normal, but it wouldn't do to encourage them. "You will do well, your grace."

The great door knocker pounded again, and they both looked toward the hall. "More visitors have arrived." She smiled up at him, and he saw the strain around her eyes.

"Are you in pain?"

"As my cousin said, it is likely false labor," she whispered. "It comes and goes."

"When did it start?"

"A few days ago, I had a spell."

"And now?"

"Now I have a bit of a backache. Please. Sit. I'll go greet our next arrivals."

He set down his untouched glass, reached for her hand and placed it over his arm. "I'll escort you. And after greeting the new arrivals, perhaps you will retire, and I might examine you?"

She laughed. "Men of action, indeed."

A large, well-tailored, but otherwise lumpy man with white hair and a ruddy complexion entered. The girl next to him wore an equally stylish blue gown that brought out the peaches and cream of her perfect complexion. Errol's heart stuttered.

Ann Strachney was here, looking as elegant as some of the ladies he'd seen shopping on Bond Street.

He straightened his spine. Why the devil was his heart racing? He'd had more than his share of women, but his heart only raced in the laboratory, or the clinic, or over a particularly well-researched journal article. Never over a girl, and certainly not over a lass who'd asked him for scientific studies and then never answered his letter. True, he'd been glad for the excuse to dispense with the promise to write, but the snub had still rankled.

REUNION

For once, Ann was grateful for Edme's tendency to squeal. Her cousin rushed to her, and, seeing her father's glower, stopped dead before them and curtsied. It hid her own attack of nerves.

"Edme." She reached for her cousin's hands and pulled her into a hug. "What a surprise. Your grace, did you invite my cousin along for the party? How very generous of you. Father, you do remember my little cousin Edme, do you not?"

Father's frown encompassed Edme but relaxed into puzzled neutrality when he took in the man yielding the duchess's arm to her husband.

Her heart thumped wildly. How handsome Errol was. His wide shoulders filled out the gray frock coat and his legs encased in dark trousers were as fine as any cavalryman's. He was as handsome as ever, and she would swear he'd grown taller, as tall as the duke.

Mrs. MacDonal flashed a smug smile. "When

Minny and I realized that Ann would be the only single young lady here, we put our heads together and decided, why not bring along her cousin? I've been given to understand, Ann, that you two haven't seen each other for years. And allow me to introduce Dr. Errol Robillard who traveled with us. Dr. Robillard, this is Mr. Strachney and you already know Ann."

Errol murmured a pleasant greeting and made the slightest of bows.

The old Errol would have smiled, even in the presence of her stuffy father.

"Here to attend to her grace, I presume," Father said.

"Dr. Robillard is our most welcome guest," the duchess said with a smile.

"Thank you, your grace," Errol said. "I'll be returning to my new practice after this, er, visit."

Ann struggled for a breath. Mr. Henderson hadn't yet conveyed to Errol the news of his one-year commitment. Perhaps a letter was chasing Errol from Edinburgh to wherever his new practice was and back to Edinburgh.

"Oh, that is a pity," Mrs. MacDonal said. "Dr. Robillard is a good Scotsman and a most particular friend of the Beecham family. Isn't that so, Edme?"

Though her remarks were directed at Edme, she smiled at Ann.

"Your other guests haven't arrived?" Father asked.

"They're all here except for Hatherot." the duke said. "Expecting him soon. Lovelace has the others in hand.

You remember George Lovelace who visited us last year? They're out shooting."

"You'll meet them at dinner." A sudden grimace flashed over the duchess's face just as the sound of the door opening drew Father's and Edme's attention. Errol and the duke exchanged a glance.

"And here is our tea," Mrs. MacDonal said, as servants carried in trays and set up another table close to the fire. "I will do the honors," she said, and followed them over.

"Thank you," the duke said. "You, my dear Fil, will go upstairs and rest." He escorted her to the door, and Errol followed.

"A man-midwife as guest. What's Kinmarty thinkin'?" Father mumbled.

"A physician, Father. The duke's thinking of his child, of course. And his wife."

"I'll expect you to dress well at dinner and wear your pearls. You ought to have brought Miss Livingston."

She swallowed her irritation and surreptitiously crossed her fingers. "What a shame she fell ill with the stomachache." Her companion's discomfort had been the result of just the right dose of salts with the Dover's powder the lady took nightly. Otherwise, she'd never have gone against Father's will. But Ann knew that, like all the other residents of Glenthistle, Miss Livingston would, after a day spent with her chamber pot, relish a break from the constant bullying. There was no danger of her dutifully appearing at Castle Kinmarty after her recovery.

"How particular a friend to the Beechams was this Robillard?" Father asked. "Haven't heard of the family before."

He was an innkeeper's son.

She wouldn't tell him that. "He was a very particular friend of the entire family. Errol spoke several languages and was quite a help to my uncle in his business."

He touched her elbow halting her. "Errol, is it?" he growled. "Look here, my dear. You're to marry a man with a title. I didn't spend years in India only to see you hitched to a man in trade."

Hitched? Her heart fluttered. Handsome, sociable, popular Errol had always been beyond her reach. Her new status as an heiress hadn't changed that. Errol had too many natural gifts to grovel for money.

From across the room, Mrs. MacDonal's shrewd gaze met hers. "Strachney," she called, "you may harangue Ann later. For now, come and join us."

She sent a grateful look to the lady and went to join her.

"And what do you say about it, Dr. Robillard?" the duchess asked.

Errol mustered his wits and tried to remember what the topic of conversation had been. Warton, the fellow across the dinner table from him, was fully engaged in attempting to draw Ann's attention while she flirted prodigiously with the man on her other side, that fellow, Lovelace.

His attention had drifted off during a discourse on holiday traditions; wasn't that it?

His hostess leaned his way. "No doubt you were thinking ahead to my ordeal."

He set down his spoon. "Aye, forgive me, your grace. I was woolgathering. You were speaking of your childhood Christmases. The Yuletide was always a busy time at my father's inn."

"Your father kept an inn?"

Soft laughter across the table drew their attention. Ann looked from side to side at her two dinner companions, pointedly ignoring his many attempts to catch her attention.

As, in truth, he'd done to her earlier before dinner, until she approached him directly.

She'd changed in the last two years. The candlelight sparked highlights of dark gold in her hair, and the smile she bestowed so generously on Lovelace lit her from the inside.

"You must have met many interesting people growing up in an inn."

He roused himself and said, "Indeed, your grace," and then was saved from further discussion when the duke, at the other end of the table rose from his seat. "My friends," he said, "I know my lady will want to withdraw soon..."

The duke and his duchess exchanged fond smiles.

"And as one member of our party will leave us in the wee hours to return to his family, I wanted to offer a farewell to my friend, George Lovelace." He signaled a footman who came round with the whisky bottle.

Lovelace was leaving? So much for Ann's flirtation with him.

"We shall miss you, Lovelace," Warton said, "but more stags for us, eh Cottingwith? And your numbers of ladies and gentlemen will be even at table, duchess."

"Don't be too certain," the duchess said.

The duke took his seat again. "As a matter of fact, we are expecting two more guests to join us. The Marquess of Hatherot will arrive any day, Highland weather permitting, and Mr. Gordon Henderson has sent word that he'll join us tomorrow for a few days."

ANN'S HANDS FROZE AROUND HER WHISKY GLASS AND SHE couldn't help looking at Errol. He frowned down at the glass he was clutching.

What did Errol know? Why was he upset? And why would Mr. Henderson travel all the way to Kinmarty? He must be coming on Mrs. MacDonal's behalf, surely not Errol's.

"Henderson is not here for the hunting, Warton. You will only have to compete with Hatherot and Cottingwith for the best stags."

Next to her, Warton laughed, as did Lovelace, but Errol's unsmiling gaze settled on her. She lifted the corners of her lips in a frozen smile and stared back.

She had no reason to be intimidated. She had helped him prodigiously, to the tune of three hundred pounds a year. She'd sacrificed, well, nothing now since Father returned from India. No, nothing now, but should she ever wish her freedom from her father, six hundred pounds would have been a great boon.

But it hadn't been wasted. It would buy help for the people here, and maybe, maybe, Errol would *want* to stay.

"To our dear friend, Lovelace." The duchess lifted her glass and then set it down. "Ladies, my husband is correct. If it's not too indelicate to say, I've been kicked and punched prodigiously through every course tonight, and I believe I shall retire."

"I'll see to our guests, Minny," Penelope said.

Errol tore his gaze away and went to help his hostess. The duke appeared and nudged him out of the way.

"I'm fine, Andrew," she said. "A good night's rest is what I need."

He dropped a kiss on her forehead. "He's fighting to get out, I suppose."

She grimaced. "Or she."

"Yes," he said, smiling down at her. "Or she. Dr. Robillard?"

"I'll see to the duchess, your grace." He glanced back at Ann and their eyes met. 'Twas no more than a moment, and yet his questioning look had her wondering what he wanted, wondering if what he wanted was her.

And then he turned, bending with natural grace to tuck the duchess's hand over his arm. Ann roused herself and joined Edme, and they followed Penelope to the drawing room, the only sound the swishing of their skirts.

. . .

It was still full dark outside when the slap of a tree branch against the window woke Ann. She slipped out of bed, grabbed a shawl, and padded to the window.

Rain had dampened the windows and stone. As she watched, a traveling chaise crept around the side of the castle.

Either Mr. Henderson was arriving, or Mr. Lovelace was leaving. She might as well get up.

The other men would be up early for hunting, but surely not yet. They'd still be abed, Errol as well, unless the duchess's time had come.

But no, though the castle was large, the room she and Edme shared was in the same wing as the duchess's, and they would have heard the commotion if her labor had started. A woman in the throes of labor could only hold back so long.

She quietly dressed in the gray light while her cousin slept on and, when a maid entered with fresh coals, she had the girl dust off her hands and help fasten the back of her gown. As she finished, Edme awakened, rubbing her eyes and demanding to know why Ann had set out her heaviest boots.

"I'm going for a walk before breakfast."

"Wait. I'm coming with you."

"Go back to bed. I can't sleep and I need time to think." If Mr. Lovelace was leaving, she'd wish him farewell. And if Mr. Henderson was arriving, she'd like to catch him alone.

"Ye're thinking too much." Edme slipped behind the screen, giggling. "Will you choose Lord Cottingwith? Or will it be Mr. Warton who will have to wait on his title? Or this marquess if he finally arrives?"

"Shush, you. I'm going to see Mr. Lovelace off. Catch up with me when you're ready."

AFTER A NIGHT OF TOSSING AND TURNING, ERROL ROSE in the dark and dressed. He'd turned his patient over to her maid after dinner and hadn't heard a peep from her since. It was too early to find breakfast laid out, but perhaps he could persuade a kitchen maid to heat up some water for tea, or even better, brew him a cup of coffee. And he could also have a look at the castle's water source and sanitation. A visit to the kitchens would tell him much.

A lamp in the entry hall cast shadows on a fanciful frieze depicting knights at battle. He heard voices and paused on the stairs.

"How *will* you manage traveling in snow if it comes, Mr. Lovelace? Should you not stay longer?"

That was Ann's voice. Errol crept lower.

Mr. Lovelace was bending over Ann's hand, and she stared up at the man, her face turned away so he couldn't see her expression. She'd wrapped herself in a heavy shawl and pulled her hair back with a ribbon. It shimmered in the lamplight.

"For your fair company, Miss Strachney, I would love to stay. But my mother has expressly asked me to spend the Yuletide with her and the children, and I'll trudge through the snow afoot if need be, for her sake."

Now she was patting Lovelace's hand.

Ann had batted her eyes at Lovelace prodigiously at dinner, and he'd heard not a mention of herbs and potions since he arrived. Had she abandoned all those interests for husband-hunting? Was she now nothing more than a flirt?

"Of course," Ann said. "She must miss your father terribly."

"She's still grieving," he said. "As are we all."

"You must, of course, go. I thought the duke would—"

"He farewelled me last night. Let him sleep, if he is able. He has an ordeal coming, remember?"

"You mean the duchess does."

"Isn't that what I said?" Lovelace placed his other hand atop hers. "The duchess will come through her confinement just fine," he said. "You know I have some experience, having nine brothers and sisters. A good midwife knows what to do…"

Errol bristled. What a jackanapes.

"But even better, the duke has brought in Dr. Robillard to see to her."

"Yes." Ann's head moved up and down, but she sounded unconvinced, and his pride took another beating. "I'll walk out with you."

He stood transfixed watching them leave.

"Errol. What are you doing up so early?"

Edme came down the steps wrapped in a heavy cloak and burdened with another.

"I could ask you the same question. Where are you going?"

"I'm joining Ann for a walk. She was in such a hurry to leave she left her cloak behind. Did you see her?"

Ann had been in a hurry to see Lovelace off.

There was no call for him to feel jealous, if that was what this was. And more than a few people thought a male physician didn't belong at a lying in. What was the old wives saying? *If the man comes, one will die.*

"No," he lied. "I'm going to go find a cup of tea and examine the castle's water source."

He took the cloak from her and tucked her hand over his arm and led her down the rest of the stairs.

"THERE YOU ARE."

Ann halted and turned to see Edme, a dark blur in her cloak, approaching.

"What are we doing out at this ridiculous hour?" Edme asked. "I've brought your cloak. Did you see Mr. Lovelace off?"

Ann slipped the heavier garment around her shoulders. "I did. Dawn is not far away. Shall we follow the path to the stables?"

"Why not?" Edme moved closer. "I've been thinking. Perhaps making Errol jealous—"

"Jealous?"

They'd had a long coze getting ready for bed the night before. Edme had teased her mercilessly about that scene in the garden when she'd fallen from the ladder.

"Errol doesn't care for me. Or would it be for your sake to spare you a match with him?"

William had proposed that idea to Edme.

Edme waved a gloved hand, brushing off the question. "Cottingwith is the highest-ranking lord here until Hatherot arrives. He's awfully dour, but perfect for the task, and in any case, you must give him due consideration. Everyone will expect it."

Her father certainly would. And if Father thought she had Errol in her sights, she'd suffer endless scolds.

She blinked. Marriage to Errol. Oh, oh, oh. Her body heated and chilled remembering the feel of his muscled chest.

It wasn't possible, not after Errol learned the truth, and it would be unthinkable to marry him without telling him she'd paid for his education.

"Don't be a goose, Edme."

Edme clutched Ann's hands, smiling. "Doona worry."

Outside, they kept to the carriage path, dodging puddles and muddy patches. Lights gleamed in the stables, and they spotted a tall figure talking with a groom. Lord Cottingwith called a greeting and came to join them.

Rain had dampened his coat, spotted his boots, and darkened the leather of his gloves, but he still made them a polite bow.

"You are wet, Lord Cottingwith," Edme exclaimed. "Have you been up and about, already? Did you encounter raindrops or were they snowflakes?"

He paused a moment and looked down his nose at

Edme. "No snowflakes, and only a few sprinkles," he finally said.

He was a solemn one. "Have you been riding already, my lord?" Ann asked.

"In the dark?" Edme exclaimed.

"I was only in the paddock. My horse had a limp yesterday and I wanted to see how he fared after a night of rest."

Another long moment passed while he again studied her cousin. "May I join you on your walk?"

Edme stepped back, her sharp chin shot up, and she tore her gaze from the tall, elegant man. "Come, Ann. Take his lordship's arm."

His lips quirked and he extended both hands. "I have two arms, Miss Beecham."

Edme's mouth opened in a look of wonder, and Ann sucked in a breath. So much for her cousin's observations on Lord Cottingwith's dourness.

Cupid was surely hiding among the bare vines climbing the stable walls. She swallowed a laugh and moved to Cottingwith's other side. "How very kind of you, my lord. There are dangerous mud puddles ahead, and we shall be happy for your escort, shall we not, Edme?"

They stepped out and spoke at length about the weather. The sky lightened enough to reveal clouds hiding the tops of the Grampian Mountains. Her second winter in the Highlands had been mild so far, but that would change.

Even a mild winter would be a hard season for those without proper shelter and fuel. While her father tried to keep her indoors, protected from visions of poverty, and hardship and of course, the weather, she found the cold invigorating, as well as the challenge of escaping her golden cage to visit the neighbors, high and low. The only neighbor she'd never met was Baron Darleton. She'd met his tenants though, and delivered them help whenever her father's back was turned.

Dodging puddles, they walked on, Lord Cottingwith's good manners carrying the conversation. With the nobleman's gaze fixed on the path ahead, Edme relaxed and joined in, blessedly leaving Ann to her thoughts.

Perhaps Edme could make a match. Her cousin's dowry was respectable.

Coming around the bend she saw a dark figure approaching and her heart jolted into a gallop.

A MARQUESS ARRIVES

"**G**ood morning," Edme called.

Errol's head shot up and his eyes widened. His gaze hopped over Edme, Lord Cottingwith, herself, and stuttered on her hand curved over his lordship's arm. Then he jerked his attention away and focused on Edme.

The scene had her flushed and dizzy. Had Mr. Henderson arrived?

Lord Cottingwith wished him a good morning, and Errol rumbled a general greeting.

Edme removed her hand and halted. "*Brrr*," she said, shivering. "I'm suddenly feeling chilled. Lord Cottingwith, will you escort me back to the Castle?"

Errol stepped forward. "I'm going that way, Edme. Allow me."

"No, Errol. I spent the entire day with you in the carriage yesterday, and you said not two words to me. His lordship has at least deigned to converse with me."

She sent him a sly smile. "You must converse with Ann."

Errol gave them a stiff smile.

The old Errol, the one Ann had watched from a distance, would have laughed heartily at Edme's impertinence and turned the jab into a joke.

Edme smiled up at her escort and reached again for his arm. "Lord Cottingwith?"

The earl glanced at Ann, his lips twitching. He wasn't humorless, and he didn't mind her cousin's forthright talk.

"For certain, you must take Edme back, my lord," Ann said.

Cottingwith bowed and placed his hand over Edme's. "Dr. Robillard, it appears we have our orders. I hope to see you at breakfast."

Errol watched them depart and turned his gaze back to her, his expression unreadable.

Feeling suddenly shy, she inhaled enough air to slow her pounding heart and found her voice. "Errol," she said. "I suppose we are trapped."

TRAPPED?

He heard the tremor in that last declaration. Why the devil should she be unsettled? Had he been that much of an ass?

He supposed he had. It was all a matter of that day in the garden when she'd landed atop him and he'd almost kissed her.

Oh hades, he had kissed her. He'd left the Beecham residence that night shaking himself for the sudden impulse that had made him do it. Even as a lad working at his father's inn, as soon as his voice changed and he sprouted whiskers, women had been drawn to him. He'd learned how to be friendly whilst avoiding entanglements. And Ann... well, until that day he'd never noticed that she'd become a woman. He hadn't wanted to write to her because he didn't want to encourage her... or maybe himself. A desirable woman who shared his keen interest in healing might distract him, and he wouldn't marry until he'd made his fortune.

"What shall we talk about?" she asked in a shaky voice.

"Perhaps..." Perhaps he should begin with the obvious. "Let us start with an apology." He hated to grovel, but in this case, he'd been in the wrong. "I ought not to have kissed you in the Beecham's garden."

She studied the graveled path. "I see."

"And I did apologize for the, er, remarks made in your cousin's study."

"The kiss was nothing, only a friendly peck. One friend comforting another. Errol, are we friends? Or can we be?"

Friends? She was a girl with an enormous dowry, one who'd been clutching the arm of an eligible earl.

"Perhaps we should leave well enough alone. Your husband will have something to say about—"

"I'm not married."

Not yet. Lord Cuttingwell—or whatever the man's name was—had looked to Ann for permission to take Edme back.

He managed a smile. "You are a rich heiress, Miss Strachney," he teased. "And I'm still a poor innkeeper's son."

She snorted. "Really? Dr. Robillard. Doctor of Medicine." She pressed her lips together. "If you wish to be formal and put on airs…" She sucked in a breath and her gaze softened. "Drat it all. I miss those years when we were all together at the Beechams. I miss the boys and the little ones. I even miss you, sometimes."

That is surely a lie. The girl who'd coerced him into writing and then didn't reply to his letter? He swallowed a spurt of anger. He could act as gentlemanly as any earl. "The rain is coming. We should get you indoors."

"I'm not some wilting flower. As you know."

He paused and studied her. The same porcelain skin in an oval face, touched by a deepening pink on her cheeks. She was beautiful.

But there were faint smudges under her eyes that hadn't been there the night before.

"You are thinner than you used to be. Paler as well," he said, improvising. "Have you been ill? Let us get you indoors."

She pressed her lips together. "Father likes to confine me indoors as well. And to be perfectly honest, he's also convinced that noblemen like their matrimonial prospects younger and more *willowy* is the word the companion he hired to torture me uses. I'm to hide the fact that I'm a spinster of almost four and twenty."

"That's absurd."

"I've been perfectly healthy." She gazed up at him and took his hand. "Unless you'd like to examine me to be sure."

He blinked and heat surged in him, his tongue tying itself up in knots. Where was the quiet mousey Ann? The Ann who'd asked him to write her about his lectures in pharmacopeia?

He glanced around. They were on a sheltered section of the path and there was no one around. He tugged her closer and watched her lips part and her eyes widen.

And remembered: she was no longer a girl abandoned to an aunt and uncle. Her father had returned. She was an heiress and he was no fortune hunter He stepped back.

She blinked, her eyes flooding with moisture. "What is wrong with you?"

"You have to ask? I wrote to you, as you requested. You never replied."

One unladylike stomp sent gravel flying. "Oh Errol." She swore an equally unladylike oath and stomped her other foot. "That *blasted* man. And you. Could you not have puzzled out why I never replied? Who was interfering? He hates me *pottering about* with herbs."

He let out a long breath. "Your father."

"A duchess doesn't work in the still room, he said.

He had Miss Lancaster hide my books and the servants follow me everywhere. I've had to… manage. Honestly, Errol. I've been starved for conversation. You must tell me everything you learned."

"I assumed…" William had said Ann was now a great heiress with plans to marry a duke.

He blinked. *This duke*, the Duke of Kinmarty. Strachney must have been furious when his plan didn't work out. He threw back his head and laughed.

"Oh Ann. William said you were to marry Kinmarty. Were you terribly disappointed?"

A smile lit her face. "Poor Father. The duchess— well she wasn't the duchess yet, not until later that evening—had taken the job as the duke's housekeeper to be closer to her cousin, Mrs. MacDonal. You should have seen my father's face when the duke had her join us for the Christmas Eve dinner."

"Your father has plans for you."

"Father has plans for everyone. He had plans for the duke, and that didn't work out."

"So, an earl will have to do?"

She wrinkled her nose. "I've grown to love the people hereabouts. I hate the thought of leaving them. Their needs are so great."

"Are there no more dukes in the area?"

"No. Though we're awaiting a new baron soon. Mayhap he'll be a prospect. Might we not consider ourselves friends until I announce my betrothal, if I ever announce my betrothal?"

Friendship was a safe option for the short time he'd

be here, but he didn't think he could be much alone with her and sustain a mere friendship. Not when she smiled at him like that.

"Let us say, until your betrothal or my departure, we will be friends. I am only here until the duchess's child is safely delivered."

A puff of breath escaped her. "And then?"

"Then I am for London. I intend to join a practice there."

"I see." She let go of his hands and turned back toward the house. "You'll become a rich and famous physician, Dr. Robillard. Attending the birth of a duke's child will be a notch on your stick. Will you specialize in childbirth?"

"No."

"Have you ever attended a birth before?"

"Yes, of course. I've also amputated limbs, set broken bones, and performed surgeries."

"It's fortunate that you could be here, since we have no one but an elderly midwife and a tippling apothecary."

"And a secret herbalist," he teased, watching her reaction. "Are you still practicing medicine, Ann?"

She shrugged and glanced at him sidewise through her dropped eyelashes. "The duke might have sent for another doctor from Edinburgh, I suppose."

The skin on his neck prickled. Why *had* the duke chosen him? He'd never received a satisfactory explanation. Hell, he'd never asked the question.

Surely the Duke of Kinmarty *was* his secret

benefactor, perhaps had taken over the charity from the last duke, else he might have called in anyone else.

He allowed himself a rueful smile. "Or he could have sent for a woman from further south. Mrs. MacDonal confided that the midwife his lady preferred —no less than a marchioness—was unavailable."

"Lady Wallenford. I have heard of her. But in any case, I'm sure you will be adequate to the task."

"Adequate?"

"Very well." Laughing, she flung out a hand in an extravagant bow. "You'll be magnificent, Dr. Robillard. No wonder the duke has asked you to attend his lady."

She'd added a smile to the teasing, one that lit up her face and sparked a desire in him to see more of this lively Ann.

That was a sobering thought. He had no means of supporting a… no, anything more than friendship was impossible.

"I suppose the real reason the duke requested me is that he's been funding my education. I'm going to make money, Ann and pay back every farthing of charity, with interest."

She ducked her head. "Perhaps it's not the duke. Perhaps it's someone else you know."

"Perhaps some other wealthy fellow? Or… perhaps it's not a *he*. That Mrs. MacDonal is a meddling sort of female." Rich as Croesus, William had said. He shuddered. "Charity from a woman." Rain pattered on the brim of his hat. "Here's the rain starting up. Come along before you are soaked and come down with a fever."

49

Errol clamped his large mitt over her dainty fingers as they hurried down the path. At least she'd had the sense to wear sturdy boots; still she seemed fragile, and in this moment, delicate.

When they reached the portico, she pulled him aside. "Errol, I have more to say to you. To... to tell you."

Thinner and paler she might be, but her lips were plump and pink, and a need to kiss her surged in him.

Behind him, the heavy oak door creaked open, and Strachney appeared, framed by the dark, like a troll emerging from his lair.

"You'll catch your death, girl. Get out of those wet clothes." He sent Errol a glare. "Their lordships will be at breakfast soon."

The loud laughter of children resounded from somewhere high in the castle.

"Those boys." Strachney growled, low in his throat. "Insists on keeping them here."

The duke's late brother's boys were in residence. The duchess mentioned that they'd have been brought down for introductions the day before, but they'd been confined to the nursery for some minor infraction.

As Ann handed over her wet cloak to a maid, the duke trotted down the stairs, scanning the grouping below.

"Ah, Strachney. Come through with me to breakfast, won't you? The rain will subside soon, and then you must join the others. Did you bring your guns?"

"I did. I've a new Purdey fowler. My man has reworked the action on it for me."

"Excellent," the duke said. "Ann," He nodded. "Dr. Robillard, come join us when you are ready."

Ann curtsied. "I'll go up and change, as you've ordered, Father."

Strachney sent one last frown and followed the duke.

When both men were out of sight, Ann let out a long breath and took Errol's arm. "Come along."

The maid had left. It was just the two of them.

"To your bedchamber? No."

She laughed. "Perhaps I'll be bold and visit yours and we may finally speak without interruption."

He opened his mouth to protest, but she shushed him and towed him up flights of stairs until she stopped on the landing. Down the corridor, a woman was singing, probably one of the maids at work.

A loud crash and a wail resounded down the far staircase. "I should see to that," he said. "Perhaps someone is hurt."

"It's the boys. Come along."

He followed her up more stairs and down another corridor into a brightly lit space at the top of the castle. Two boys sprawled on the floor, toy soldiers grouped in front of them. A dark-haired, dark-skinned woman swathed in a colorful sari looked up from a chair, while her counterpart, a fair-haired young servant girl in a drab gown rose from her mending.

"Ann," the smaller boy squealed, and the other

shouted a greeting. Both boys flung themselves into her arms.

So, it was true. The duke had taken in his brother's by-blows born of a native woman during his time in India. It was only a minor scandal, but had been another reason William had hesitated about allowing Edme to visit Castle Kinmarty.

They were cheerful, mischievous boys, and clearly had charmed Ann. "Ravi, Arun, meet Dr. Robillard, come to help your aunt when the baby comes. And Errol, this is Sitara, a cousin, come from India to help look after these wild ones. And now I must go change into something dry. I won't be but a moment."

"Come and see my soldiers," Ravi said, tugging on his hand.

"Wait a moment. I heard a wail earlier," Errol said. "Has someone been injured?"

"Yes. A whole regiment of my troops were wiped out," Arun cried, and from her place on the chair, their cousin chuckled.

"Well, then," he said, getting down on his knees. "Perhaps I can tend to their wounds."

HER NERVES ON EDGE, ANN DONNED ONE OF HER newest morning gowns, a sky-blue wool with embroidered trim and climbed the stairs back to the nursery. Errol had been more cordial to her than ever before. It was no use hoping they could be more than friends, but she prayed that they could remain on good terms after she told him everything. If she could but get up the nerve to do so.

In the nursery doorway, she heard his rich baritone. The boys had returned to their play, and he was speaking with Sitara, who smiled and greeted Ann and went back to her needlework.

"I've come to guide you to the breakfast room," Ann said, leading him out. "I daresay you won't know where it is."

"I found my way to the kitchens this morning."

"Did you? Well done."

"With some help. A tweeny sent me in the right direction, and I followed my nose the rest of the way."

They descended two floors, headed down a corridor, took a short flight of stairs up, and turned more corners before descending another staircase. "I still sometimes get lost in the Castle," Ann said.

Double doors stood open at the end of a corridor, and the reassuring smells of bacon, fresh scones, kidneys, baked beans, and haggis led them into the room.

As the duke welcomed them, Ann scanned the table. Her father's frown at seeing her still in company with Errol was to be expected, as was Mr. Warton's friendly greeting. Lord Cottingwith's head was bent toward Edme, who sent Ann a dazed smile. Mr. Henderson had not arrived, thank goodness.

A man appeared and bowed before her with a glittering smile that made her catch her breath. He was quite the handsomest man she'd ever seen, in his own way, with a head of golden curls, sapphire blue eyes, a strong, straight nose and square jaw. He was, like the other younger men, dressed to leave immediately for hunting in tweeds, trousers, and top boots.

He bowed over her hand. "Allow me to be so bold as to introduce myself, since mine host is not doing the honors."

The duke's rumbling laugh reached them. "Miss Strachney, Dr. Robillard, this fellow pushing himself forward is the estimable Marquess of Hatherot. Hatherot, Miss Strachney of Glenthistle, and Dr. Errol Robillard."

He beamed another smile that left her feeling as dazed as Edme seemed to be, nodded to Errol, and led her off to a seat at the table and claimed the one next to it for himself.

She glanced back at Errol but he'd turned away and was filling a plate.

Hatherot pushed her chair in. "I'll fetch you some breakfast. A little of everything, I think."

She nodded, distracted. Across the table, Father's eyes glittered. Oh, he was mentally rubbing his hands together anticipating a marquess in the family and calculating the financial value of that connection. Father's aspirations were not entirely a matter of social climbing. He wanted power and money.

She accepted the plate—indeed it was a little of everything. Miss Lancaster would have told her to take only a piece of buttered toast. She picked at the food and set about making small talk with the marquess and checking on Errol when father was turned away.

The way Errol refused to meet her eyes told her he

might, possibly, maybe, be jealous. No one had ever been jealous on her behalf before.

She shared a look with Edme. Lord Cottingwith was discussing shooting with the duke, and Edme had shed some of her dazzlement. Ann's Adonis continued pouring out charm like treacle from a bottomless pitcher.

Errol ate quickly and issued a general farewell, leaving Ann feeling bereft and anxious.

ERROL HEADED DOWN THE CORRIDOR, HOPING TO CHECK on his patient. The sooner the child arrived, the sooner he would leave Kinmarty. He had no wish to hang about watching that golden lord woo Ann.

He tried to shake off the creeping jealousy and his damnable pride. He'd written to her, sharing tidbits from his pharmacy lectures. Not that he wanted to encourage her dabbling in herbals, but it was a harmless enough pursuit for a woman, wasn't it? And it was pleasant to speak with someone who thought about the healing possibilities of medicines, instead of how much they could be sold for.

When she didn't bother to reply, he'd swallowed his pride, put her out of his mind, and devoted himself to his studies. Though he had proved his abilities in the surgery, he'd ruffled some feathers by wholeheartedly embracing the notion of improved sanitation. He'd had to prove himself better than most and navigate the vanities of professors in hopes of graduating and finding a good position. The call to London had been a godsend. With a few years of hard work, he'd be able to buy a home and support a wife and children.

The duchess had breakfasted in her room and then gone to the drawing room, her maid said. When he pushed through the door, he suppressed a groan. The only occupant was Benedict Strachney.

AN UNEXPECTED BEQUEST

Strachney looked up, his complexion an unhealthy shade of orange, his eyes bulging. His edema was likely caused by a poor heart, an improper diet, or some other illness. Errol couldn't be sure without a thorough examination. One he wouldn't offer the pompous old arse.

"Good day to you, sir," he said. "I was told I might find the duchess here."

"She just left."

"Do you know where she went?"

"No. You're the one, aren't you?"

"I beg your pardon."

"You wrote to her. Without my permission. I heard about you. Son of a black innkeeper, and a particular friend of the family. I won't have it, you know."

His pulse pounded in his ears, and he knew his color must be rising along with the heat of his anger.

He leveled a steady gaze at the man, shoving his ire aside. He'd dealt with Strachney's sort of pompous fool before, and if he expected to be a success in London, he'd deal with this sort again.

And he'd do it without groveling. He was a physician, a man of education, his honorable father's son. He was worthy of respect. "You won't have what, Strachney?"

"My daughter will have a title. If you think to have her money—well, she'll marry a man I approve of, or there'll be none, and she can starve in a garret in some overcrowded rookery."

An invisible hand gripped his heart. He'd visited flats like that, in Edinburgh's old town, crowded with sick, starving wraiths.

"A title or death? That is the choice you'd force on your only child? What sort of honorable man would do that?"

"My influence runs far. If you think to defy me, I can—I will—ruin you."

He hadn't thought to defy the man. No matter how often his thoughts went to kissing Ann, he knew their friendship could never be a romance.

Had everyone thought that it was? Did Ann think that?

Would he mind if she did? Ann was lovely, and kind, and... living with this man, what had her life become? Gentle, sweet Ann, how had she tolerated him?

He had very little, but if they married...

He shook off the unexpected thought. He was losing his mind. "How far does your influence run, Strachney? India, perhaps, given that you lived there for so long. But the Americas? The Antipodes? Physicians are needed all over the world."

Strachney's face flamed, blood vessels popping. He looked very near to an apoplexy. Errol didn't care. "Your daughter and I—"

"Lay a hand on her and I'll—"

"I would *never* hurt Ann." His hands balled into fists. "And if I ever hear that *you* harm her in *any* way, I'll thrash you within an inch of your life."

"Why you…" Strachney spluttered and sank into a chair swiping a shaking hand through his thatch of white hair.

Shame crept over Errol. He was a doctor, for God's sake, a healer. No longer the brawling son of a tavernkeeper. Not that he ever had done much more than tossing out the troublesome inn patrons, but those days were past. "Are you ill, Mr. Strachney?"

"*Blast you*, I'm angry."

"Your color is high, your hands are trembling, and you're swollen with fluid. Is your heart giving out? I can provide you the name of a good man in Edinburgh."

"Get out."

"Gladly."

Closing the door behind him, Errol paused in the corridor and braced a hand on the wainscoting. For the old man to be so angry… Did Ann care for Errol in that way?

What a dunderhead he was not to realize it had been her father interfering with Ann's correspondence.

His spirits lifted. He had a profession. He had a

position in London. He'd only thrown out that bit about the Antipodes to rile her father. He'd be back in London soon. Once he'd established himself, he could return for her and…

But during that time, even if she stayed at Kinmarty, she'd be plagued by her bullying father. And he'd just behaved abominably toward the man.

"Ah, there you are, Doctor Robillard. Are you quite well?"

The duchess studied him, her arms folded over her expansive abdomen.

"Your grace." He straightened. "Yes. I'm, er, well."

Her gaze shifted to the closed door. "Is Strachney still within?"

"Yes."

She took his arm and they headed down a corridor. "Poor Strachney. I would feel sorrier for him, if he wasn't such a tyrant. He had a great disappointment last year, you know. He'd planned for Ann to marry the duke, whereupon his daughter would become a duchess and he would use his wealth to control Kinmarty and squeeze a few more farthings out of the land and the people here."

Astonished that she would confide in him—and the contents of that confidence, he paused.

"I've rendered you speechless, Dr. Robillard. You're thinking that I'm vulgar."

"No, no, duchess. I have no standing to do so. I'm… surprised is all. Gaining the title for Ann would not have been enough for him?"

She shook her head. "No. He misjudged Andrew

most dreadfully. My husband was never expecting the title, you know. It ought to have gone to his brother, Evan, Penelope's late husband. Strachney knew Kinmarty was in financial difficulties, and he thought to use his wealth to manipulate and be the true power in this little realm." She laughed. "But by the time he and Ann paid their first visit, the duke and I had fallen hopelessly in love. I had no money, but Penelope had gobs of it. And not ill-gotten off the backs of Indian laborers, either. Evan had served valiantly in some local prince's army and been handsomely rewarded."

"And the children?" He couldn't help asking.

She shrugged. "By his second wife."

"I've... er... heard that such a thing is not uncommon there."

She gave him a merry smile. "We don't call them wives, but it is not so uncommon here, either. Though not for the Duke of Kinmarty; not while I'm his duchess."

Best to change the subject. "And how are you feeling today?"

"Like a tired whale. Or perhaps an elephant is a better comparison. Penelope rode on elephants you know and found it quite exhilarating."

He saw it then: she was chattering on because she was unsettled and trying to hide it. "You mustn't tax yourself. Forgive me, but I've been wondering why you planned a house party during your confinement."

"We are hosting the gentlemen primarily for business. Strachney got wind of unmarried lords and wangled an invitation for him and Ann. And to vex him, Penelope brought Edme along. We plan to charge a very large fee for shooting parties, and these men will help us find paying guests. It was Lovelace's idea. For my part, I'm glad we'll have a proper surgeon when one of these fools shoots himself in the foot. I'm ever so glad you're here, Dr. Robillard. In fact, I would love you to say you'd like to stay longer. Do you shoot?"

"No, duchess, I'm more of a fisherman. I grew up in Edinburgh. My father was an innkeeper. I'd no access to shooting."

"I see. Well, come, let me show you the library. I've been working for the past several months to clean and catalogue the volumes. Perhaps we shall find some other way to persuade you to stay."

As she was showing him the arrangement of the library shelves, the duke entered and joined them, inquiring about her health.

"I'm quite well, Andrew. No true pains yet."

Errol swept a gaze over her. "It may yet be several more days."

"In that case, Robillard, I should like to take you away tomorrow and introduce you to some of the locals, if my dear wife will allow it."

"Of course," the duchess said. "Babies take their time, I hear. I can always send for both of you if needed."

"I'll introduce you to my factor—ah, here is Forbes now."

Forbes, a sturdy white-haired man in his sixties or perhaps even older, greeted them.

"Forbes was the butler at Kinmarty when I was a

child. He knows every inch of the castle and the surrounding countryside. He's found a cottage in the village that he thinks will suit as a surgery. Perhaps we can look at it tomorrow."

A cottage and surgery. Something permanent. What was the duke up to? The last thing he wanted was to become firmly established here.

The duchess patted his arm. "I'll be all right, Dr. Robillard."

He dipped his head. Let her think that his reluctance had to do with worrying about her condition.

"We'll leave word where we're going," Forbes said. "Duke, I've put Mr. Henderson in your study."

"He's arrived then. I'll just go and greet him."

"'Struth, your grace, it's Dr. Robillard he's asked for."

All eyes turned his way. "He wrote that he wanted to meet with me here. I thought it was odd. I stopped at his office in Edinburgh and none of his clerks would say why."

"It's surely good news then," said the duke, a guileless look on his face.

"What news, Andrew?" the duchess asked.

The duke shrugged. "Look on the bright side, I always say. Forbes, show Dr. Robillard the way, will you?"

SOMEONE HAD TAKEN GREAT CARE WITH THE DUKE'S study, a small room tucked away at the back of the house. The room smelled of lemon oil, tobacco, and wood smoke, and the aged desk and cabinets had been polished to a high shine. Deep green curtains framed the windows, and the same fabric covered the padded seats of the wooden armchairs and two wing chairs by the hearth. A few pieces of mail sat to one side of the dust-free desktop and in the middle was a stack of folders holding papers.

Henderson rose to greet him. A man of middling age, short of stature, and immaculately clad in sober dark coats and sparkling white neckcloth, he came around the desk and shook Errol's hand, congratulating him on finishing his schooling.

"Glad I am that I found you," Henderson said, "and lucky that the duke needed your services in Kinmarty at the same time I had business here."

"I see," Errol said. The duke had arranged all of this. That was telling. Surely the duke was his anonymous benefactor. "Well, get on with it then, if you would, please. Two matters of business, you said. I suppose one of them might have to do with my benefactor. I've sent over all the expense reports from my schooling. I trust all is to your satisfaction?"

Henderson returned to his seat behind the desk and placed a hand on the files. "Yes, you fulfilled your studies and the expense reporting requirements most admirably. We shall get to that matter anon. But first, I must tell you about your grandfather Barclay Callum's legacy."

His grandfather, Barclay Callum? His father's father

was long dead. This must be his mother's father. "Legacy?"

"Yes. You didn't know about it? I'm not surprised. We had a devil of a time chasing down who the heir was, but I'm happy to see the estate and title go to a man of principle and accomplishment."

The estate? His legs and ankles tingled, and his hands grew clammy. His grandfather had held a title? Though he'd never learned so much as the man's name, he knew he was a hot-tempered, foul-mouthed, stingy old man— or so he'd learned from his parents' whispered conversations. Upon his daughter's marriage to an Edinburgh innkeeper, the old man had raged at the world and cut her off. She'd somehow kept in touch with her poor long-suffering mother though, and when that lady's death neared, his mother had gone home to tend her.

"Dr. Robillard, you are now Baron Darleton."

The carved frieze on the desk front rippled, and his fingers curled around the chair arms. *"Baron Darleton."*

"Yes. I'm told there was an estrangement between him and your mother. There was no entail, and this being a Scottish barony, he might have left all to someone else. But the old baron had a change of heart in his last years. Now," Henderson slid papers out of the top folder," I've gone over the books and inventories with your granddad's factor, Mr. Busby."

Errol strained to understand as the solicitor droned on about furnishings, livestock, servants, and tenants. The estate tax would be minimal; when his wife and daughter died, the old man had devoted himself to the bottle and, despite the factor's efforts, there was very little money left.

"He let the property go to hell," Errol said. "Was the factor stealing?"

"Not that I've been able to find. It appears he scraped along barely keeping up the crofts. There are a few longtime tenants left, though their cottages need repairs, as do the barns, stables, and other outbuildings. And of course, the castle, Mounth Tower."

Mounth Tower. He'd never known the name of the place, but his mother was buried there, that much he knew.

"It's no more than an hour's ride from Kinmarty. I'll escort you there and introduce you to Busby and the servants."

Memories rushed him of the last time he saw his mother and of her tender farewell. His father had reluctantly allowed her to go—as if he thought he could restrain his high-spirited wife.

As it turned out, Da had been right. The visit had killed her.

He wanted to see her grave. As for the rest of it—he was a *baron*. Would that impress his new employers? Could the factor maintain the property while the new Baron Darleton took up his practice in London?

"Shall we visit there today?" The sooner the better.

"I fear I'm not free until the morrow. I have other business here at Kinmarty today." Henderson extracted another folder from his stack. "Now, here are your copies of the estate documents and inventories. You may wish to review those today, and we'll go over the ledgers with Busby tomorrow."

Errol stood and reached for the documents, and then remembered the solicitor's letter arranging this appointment. "What was the second matter of business, Mr. Henderson?"

"Ah yes." He rose from his chair as well. "If you recall there was a stipulation made by your benefactor that you provide medical services for one year after completion of your studies."

He'd had a handshake agreement with Beecham to serve the warehouse staff for a time. Had something more formal been included by his second benefactor? He'd been in such a desperate lather, he may have missed that stipulation.

Well, he'd easily find a way to hand off that task to another graduate, someone who didn't want to take up the thankless job of ship's doctor in the navy. "Go on."

"A contractual agreement it was."

"To serve Beecham's employees and their families at the warehouse in Edinburgh?"

The solicitor blinked. "No. In point of fact, the requirement was for you to serve one year as directed by the benefactor upon completion of your studies. And the requirement is one year of service as physician in Kinmarty."

He plopped down in the chair. A year in the Highlands? His mind raced through the names of his university classmates. Who could he pay off to spend a year of his life in this godforsaken place?

"I've accepted a position with a practice in London,"

he said. "Tell me, Henderson, if I pay back the benefactor, will that nullify that requirement?"

"That was not a stipulation of the contract, but you can certainly make the proposal."

"Is there enough cash in the Darleton estate—"

"No, I'm afraid not." Henderson paused, frowning. "Since there's no entail, you could sell the castle and land, and the title with it. I *have* received an inquiry from an interested buyer. But, I can't emphasize enough, you must see the property first. It is, after all, your family legacy, and if you must stay, you can easily live at Mounth Tower and run a practice in the village." Henderson examined his watch. "Do review those documents. I trust I will see you at dinner?"

It was a clear enough dismissal by the little solicitor. "Who is the interested buyer?" he asked.

"That I don't know. The inquiry came through another solicitor. Dr. Robillard, I have some more business to attend to, but I'll be happy to answer any questions you have after reviewing those documents. Perhaps on the ride over to Mounth Tower tomorrow?"

Errol rose heavily and tucked the folder under his arm. Henderson saw him to the door and closed it behind him. Halfway up the stairs to his well-appointed bedchamber with its writing desk, he realized—he hadn't asked Henderson the name of his benefactor.

No doubt it was the duke. He turned around and descended the stairs and learned from a footman that the duke was in the factor's office.

After stumbling down wrong corridors and making wrong turns, he finally reached a humbler door on the ground level, and Forbes answered. From his chair by the fire, the duke called out a greeting.

The factor's office was a smaller version of the duke's study, with identical curtains and upholstery, but only one wing chair by the fire, where the duke was sprawled.

Kinmarty sat up and lifted a glass. An inch of amber liquid shimmered in the firelight. "Join us, Robillard. For heaven's sake, sit down, man, and pour him some, Forbes."

"Have a drink and tell us what you think. Forbes and I have established a distillery." He laughed. "A legal one."

"The water of life?"

"Yes. '*Uisge Beatha.*' I understand your father kept a drinking establishment."

"Yes, and a good-sized inn as well. He himself was more given to the rum, being that his father was a man from the West Indies."

Forbes slid a wooden chair over and then handed him a tumbler.

"Sit man, and drink," the duke said. "You've had a shock."

He sighed and took a sip. The smooth liquid coursed through him with a reviving warmth.

"Well?" Kinmarty asked.

"It's good."

"All credit goes to Forbes, the master distiller."

He tipped back the glass and drained the rest of it and found Kinmarty watching him.

"You knew about Darleton," Errol said.

"Yes. Henderson told me in confidence, but Forbes and I are the only ones who know. Not even the Darleton factor knows the name of the heir. The estate is in bad repair, I'm afraid. I would congratulate you, but I believe I know what you're feeling right now. I didn't expect to inherit Kinmarty."

"I'd appreciate it if you continue to keep this matter quiet until I visit the estate," Errol said. "There's an interested buyer. Is it you, your grace?"

Kinmarty laughed. "Good Lord, no. I've had to humble myself by letting a *woman*, my sister-in-law Penelope, invest in Kinmarty. I sooth my conscience by telling myself she ought to have been the duchess here. I don't have funds to buy your estate."

"Might the buyer be Mrs. MacDonal?"

"Henderson didna give you more of a hint who it is?" Forbes asked.

"He told me another solicitor approached him and wouldn't give the name."

The two men shared a look. Kinmarty shrugged. "Well then, it's not Penelope. Henderson works for her."

"I have another question, your grace. The last two years of my university fees and expenses were paid by an anonymous benefactor. Was that person you?"

"I've only been duke for a little over a year."

"Perhaps the old duke?"

"No. And not Penelope either, if that's your next

question, because she only returned from India a year ago. Why do you ask?"

"I ask because you and Forbes want to show me a cottage you've designated for a surgery, and because I've just learned that my anonymous benefactor requires me to forgo a plum position in London and serve one year as Kinmarty's physician."

Forbes cleared his throat. "Dr. Robillard, I've been trying these last months to entice a medical man here. I only ask your help in letting me know if the place will suit. If ye'll stay, that'll be grand, but if not, if ye can help us find a doctor, that would be grand as well."

"We'd be lucky to have you," the duke said. "Professor Monro said you had the deftest hands of any of the surgeons he'd trained and a good head for diagnosis. Good with maternity complications as well. I can see why you'd be wanted in London."

"I wondered why you'd asked for me," he said.

"Andrew, I wondered where you got off to." The duchess stood in the open doorway and the three men shot out of their seats.

Kinmarty grinned and went to put his arm around her. "Only the best for my duchess. I was telling Dr.Robillard why we asked for his services, my love."

"Ah. Strachney is roaming about the castle, and the shooting party has returned. You must go and entertain them. I'm in no condition to do so."

"Are you feeling unwell?" Errol asked.

She waved a hand. "I've spent the morning finishing the nursery preparations, with Edme and Ann's help. I'll go have a rest before dinner."

"I'll escort you, Fil," the duke said. "You must show me this nursery. Robillard, I'll leave you to review whatever document it is you're holding."

"Very well. Send for me if you need me, your grace. I'll be in my room."

"YE'RE DAWDLING, CUZ," EDME SAID, TAKING A JEWELED hairclip from Ann's hand. "The marquess will be waiting for ye."

Ann rolled her eyes at the reflection in the mirror. Since his return from the morning's shooting, Hatherot had dogged her through an afternoon when she'd been hoping to speak with Mr. Henderson.

"Is he a fortune hunter, then?" Edme asked.

Ann scoffed. "What do you think?"

"That he's smitten with ye?" Edme said. "But what a handsome, braw fellow to have chasing ye."

"Chasing my dowry, you mean."

Edme loosened a tendril of hair at each side of Ann's face. "I'll grant ye your dowry is a draw, but ye're quite lovely when ye're not frowning. Ye noticed, I hope, that I stayed faithfully by your side when the gentlemen came in for tea."

She recalled her father's words in the carriage. *Should any man importune you, only make sure it is one of the single men of high station and we shall have you wed by Hogmanay.*

If only Errol would importune her again.

He would be at dinner and so would Mr.

Henderson. She found her shawl and hurried her cousin out the door.

ON HIS WAY TO DINNER, ERROL ENCOUNTERED Henderson in the corridor and exchanged greetings.

"Fine weather we're having for December," Henderson said.

Setting the boundaries of the conversation, Errol assumed. They'd have a more private conversation the next day on the ride to Darleton.

"I hope it holds," Henderson added. "I've promised my wife I'll arrive in time for Christmas."

Errol groped around for a polite response that wasn't too inane. "You're returning to Edinburgh?"

"Ah, no, I'm for Inverness and a family gathering there."

As they entered the drawing room, the duke waved a greeting. Mr. Warton and Cuttingwell nodded. The newest arrival, the Marquess of Hottentot, or whatever his name was, curled his lip in a dismissive glance and turned back to his conversation with Strachney.

Strachney turned a curious gaze on Henderson.

The duke beckoned them, poured drinks, and made introductions. Errol stepped back and listened while the men discussed hunting. The marquess watched the door like a hawk, and when the ladies walked in, all four of them together, his face lit up in a bright smile. He went to claim Ann but, wedged between Mrs. MacDonal and Edme, Ann steered both ladies over to where Mr. Henderson stood, like himself another outsider on the edge of this aristocratic circle.

Henderson greeted Mrs. MacDonal and Ann—as if he knew Ann already. Ann introduced Edme.

Strachney cleared his throat loudly. "And why are you here at Kinmarty, Henderson?" he called.

A hush fell over the room. The marquess chuckled. "Excellent question, Strachney. We have sportsmen, a neighbor, and a doctor. Which of those groups do you fall into, Henderson? Do satisfy our curiosity, if you will."

The ass. Errol glanced over and saw that Ann's smile had faded, and color rose in her face.

"Henderson is a most esteemed Edinburgh solicitor," said the duke, "and our guest."

Mrs. MacDonal laughed. "And I feel certain Mr. Henderson does not discuss his clients around the dinner table."

"I do not indeed, ma'am," Henderson said with an affable smile. "Or anywhere else."

"And how do you know my daughter?" Strachney asked.

A VISIT TO MOUNTH TOWER

$\mathcal{A}$nn felt the squeeze of Penelope's hand on her arm. "Mr. Henderson arrived this morning. Ann and I met him earlier today, of course."

She sent Penelope a grateful smile, while the lady continued with her easy grace. "Come, Mr. Henderson, sit down and entertain us ladies with your plans to travel on to Inverness."

"Yes, I should like to hear as well," Hatherot said.

Ann glanced back at Errol and caught his frown. And then she noticed her father scowling at her—because he'd seen her glance at Errol.

A jittery feeling rose in her. Was Errol jealous of Hatherot? Or had Henderson told him that she'd paid his university fees?

Loosened by the good Kinmarty whisky, the normally sober solicitor spun stories about the family's Yuletide celebrations in years past. The marquess, probably seeing no contest in the middle-aged man, joined the conversation with less sneering and more cordiality. Across the room, her father relaxed. Errol, however, turned away and took a seat near the duchess.

She'd get no moment alone with Henderson this night.

FROM HER WINDOW THE NEXT MORNING, ANN SAW Errol ride off with the duke and Mr. Henderson.

So much for having a longer talk with either man alone. When she and Edme went down to breakfast, she found that all the men had left already to go shooting—her father included. The duchess was breakfasting in her room, but Penelope soon joined them and set out the plans for holiday decorations. If the weather held, they'd gather boughs in two days' time and have the men find a suitable yule log.

Christmas was only a few days away. She hoped Errol would still be here.

"Ann," Penelope asked with a sly grin, "what do you think of the courtship rituals?"

Edme giggled and Penelope joined in.

Ann shuddered. The marquess was making his intentions very clear. "I've never truly been pursued before."

"No, not *that* courtship," Penelope said. "I mean the one between Hatherot and your father."

Edme snickered again, but Ann set down her fork. "Oh, what am I to do?" she said. "He's a fortune hunter, isn't he?"

"Pockets to let. A great gambler, and always loses.

He was organizing a card game last night after we retired. They've gone out so early, it must not have lasted long."

"Or he was behaving himself in front of my father."

"Ye must tell your father this," Edme said. "Though he is very handsome."

"He is that," Penelope said. "And clever enough to hold an intelligent conversation."

"Did you know him before?" Ann asked.

"No. But I've met plenty of men like him. He's rather like my late husband." She paused with a faraway look. "We didn't invite him, you know. He weaseled his way in by promising to support Andrew's hunting endeavor. He's an acquaintance of Warton. I suspect Warton mentioned the presence of a great heiress."

"So, Mr. Warton isn't to be trusted either," Ann said.

"Are all noblemen so deceptive?" Edme mused.

Penelope studied her toast. "Not Cottingwith, I think. Though one can't be sure until one has them investigated."

Edme's color was rising. She glanced away, bit her tongue, and sent Ann a twinkling look. "And not Errol, either. Of course, he's not a lord like the earl and marquess, nor a lord-in-waiting like Mr. Warton. He wants to work for a living. Da always trusted him and so do my brothers."

"And there you have the advantage," Penelope said. "You've known Dr. Robillard all your life and your brothers vouch for him. Though we don't know what your brothers get up to when they're away from the ladies."

Edme giggled again and Ann forced a laugh. The thought of Errol getting up to anything with other women made her blood run cold and she suddenly felt sick.

"I'm finished, I think." She excused herself and hurried out before she had to decide where she was going.

Deciding she needed fresh air, she hurried to her room, changed to her heavy boots, found her mantle, and fled down the lane, away from the stables where she might encounter the men who were hunting.

Halfway down, she saw a young boy racing up the lane.

"Rolly." She hurried to meet him.

"M-miss," he said huffing, his dirty cap askew. The tattered boots were far too big for him and deeply padded with dirty cloths.

"Catch your breath," she said. "What is wrong?"

"It's me mam. He's walloped her. Kin ye come?'

The Gillespies croft was thirty minutes at least by carriage. The lad must have been running for nigh on two hours.

"Wait here."

Keeping her fingers crossed the men were still out, she ran to the stables. Long minutes later, she yanked the lad up onto the gig beside her and they were off.

"Now then, is your da still at home?"

"Nay. He's gone off to…" He swiped at his eyes.

To drink. Rolly didn't have to say more. "I don't have my medicines, but I'll see what I can do."

She would bring Maggie Gillespie back to the castle, if need be. She felt certain the duke wouldn't mind.

And Errol could tend to her, if treating a crofter living in less than sanitary conditions wasn't beneath him.

PENELOPE MACDONAL HANDED AROUND CUPS OF TEA IN Minny's sitting room. "Where is Ann, Edme?" she asked. "I haven't seen her since breakfast."

"I don't know. I thought she would be here with you, your grace," Edme said. "She wasn't in our room."

Penelope exchanged a look with Minny. Ann had rushed from the breakfast room hours ago. "Andrew is back with Mr. Henderson. The others will be back from hunting soon. Has Dr. Robillard returned?"

A knock on the door tapped out a pattern she recognized. "Will you excuse me? Edme, take over here, please."

Urjit, her loyal servant—more than a servant, her dearest friend—nodded and led her along the corridor away from the footman on duty.

"Miss Strachney took a gig out this morning in a great hurry. Rolly Gillespie was seen climbing up with her."

"Have the stable saddle my horse."

"Our horses," he said.

"Yes. Thank you, my friend." She snatched the first

maid she came to away from her dusting and hurried to change into her riding habit. Rolly Gillespie's father was a bad piece of work. If Ann went to that croft alone, she was in danger.

Errol might find her, of course, but what if she returned to Kinmarty alone with him?

She chuckled. If that happened, she'd love to see the look on Strachney's face.

But Errol might not find her in time.

"My mother's married name, Robillard, must be added," he told Busby.

The factor scribbled in his notebook.

"See that the stonemason gets on to it immediately."

"Of course. Anything else here, sir?"

He looked around. Busby had a long list of chores in his notebook from their tour of Mounth Tower. The family graveyard, however, appeared to have been well tended, almost lovingly cared for.

His mother's grave lay next to his grandmother's. Bare soil on the other side was all that could be seen of his grandfather's final resting place.

"Have him carve the old baron's stone before we lose sight of where he was buried."

Busby scribbled some more.

A chill wind nipped him, and he looked at the sky. The midafternoon sun had disappeared behind clouds. More rain was coming.

And he had one more stop before returning to Kinmarty.

The duke and Henderson had left earlier, and he knew that a groom on a fast horse could fetch him back quickly if the duchess needed him. Still, he shouldn't linger long.

Both men mounted and Busby led him down a track from the house. He could hear the water before he saw it. As they broke through the trees, he saw figures scrambling away through the brush.

"Poachers?" he said.

"Hungry crofters likely. We try to keep them away. The old baron lost interest those last few years." Busby cleared his throat. "Finest salmon fishing in all of Scotland here."

"Is there a lodge around here?" he asked. "Any dwellings nearby that could be turned into lodges?"

"Nearest croft is the Gillespies. That way." Busby pointed. "Two rooms. Dirt floor. Needs a new roof."

Darleton's property inventory listed several such crofts.

The river rushed down and widened into a deep natural pool, and then rushed on down to the sea miles away. "I wish I'd brought gear," he said.

"I'll fetch some, if you'd like."

Errol shook his head. "Another time. It's getting late." He'd find time to fish on his land before he sold it. And he would have to sell it. He couldn't see a way to make Darleton self-supporting. Even if fishing brought in funds, he didn't have the capital to establish such a business, or the time to do so if he returned to London.

He bid the factor farewell and promised to return as soon as his business at Kinmarty allowed.

He turned down a path in the direction Busby had pointed, hoping he'd get a glimpse of this two-room hovel on his way to the lane.

As he came over a rise, he saw it.

Dear God, his father's worst nags had been sheltered better than these people who depended on him. But a respectable gig and horse stood in front and as he watched, a woman in a blue mantle stepped out of the hovel.

It was Ann.

A man roared, and he spotted a burly fellow loping through a patch of trees.

Errol spurred his horse. The man saw him, stopped, and took off back running the other way. He turned to give chase, but Ann shouted for Errol to stop.

Dismounting, he went to her. A scrawny young boy with a dirty cap peeked from behind her.

"Ann, what are you—"

"Come," she said, beckoning him.

Inside, a small peat fire fought the chill air rustling in through the roof and the tattered blankets covering the windows. A tallow candle sat on the only table, and the only chair held a sturdy-framed woman.

"Maggie," Ann said, "this is Dr. Robillard. I've done what I can, but can you have a look at her, Errol?"

The woman struggled to rise, but he nudged her back and went down on one knee. Both of her eyes were blackened, and near swollen shut.

"Are you Mrs. Gillespie?" he asked.

She nodded.

"Who did this to you?" he asked.

"Me da," the boy said.

"Shush, Rolly. He's not a bad man when he's not drinking."

"Did he hit you anywhere else?"

She shook her head.

"Your hand, Maggie," Ann said softly. "I can't tell if it's broken."

He lifted her right hand. The knuckles were raw, the thumb joint swollen. He had her wiggle her fingers, make a fist, and then probed every joint. It didn't seem broken, and there wasn't much he could do if it was, except to wrap it.

"I suppose you hit him back," he said.

"Aye. Had to."

"Was that your da running to the house like a madman?" he asked the boy.

"Aye."

"We're taking you somewhere safe, Mrs. Gillespie," Errol said, and heard Ann expel a breath.

He got to his feet. The old housekeeper at Mounth Tower might protest, and Gillespie might cause trouble there. Perhaps he could take her and the boy further away, to Kinmarty.

"I'm not leavin' me home," she said, wobbling up from the chair. "It's her, Miss Strachney, as gets him riled. Her being here and seeing our troubles. And now ye show up from nowhere. He don't like strangers aboot. Now, please, sir, I thankee, but I've no money to pay a doctor."

He opened his mouth to tell her he was no stranger, but her new laird, and thought better of it. If he sold

Darleton, these people's problems would be someone else's.

"Rolly oughtn't have gone for ye, miss."

"Don't you dare lay a hand on him, Maggie Gillespie," Ann said. "Come, Errol."

The lad followed them out, and Ann pulled him aside. "Be good for your mam. But don't let her allow him to hurt you. If your da comes after you, you run like the wind. If you can't find me, go to the duke. He'll help you."

Errol tied his horse to the back of the gig and joined her on the seat.

Ann straightened her skirts and pressed into the seat rail. And still, the crush of his big body on the too small bench did strange things to her. Every bump sent a current of electricity through her hip, and arm, and shoulder.

"The boy came for you?" he asked.

"Yes."

"Does that happen often?"

"No, but he knows I'll help him if I am able. I'd like to check on him more but... I've convinced my father that a true lady visits tenants and helps the poor, but he puts limits on me."

"The Gillespies are not your father's tenants."

She turned and looked at his strong, grim profile. He was staring straight ahead, navigating a muddy stretch of lane. How would he know the Gillespies weren't Glenthistle tenants? He'd left early with

Henderson and the duke, without leaving word of their destination.

Surely the duchess would have known where he'd gone. She ought to have asked before she left the castle.

"What were *you* doing out here?" she asked.

He shot a quick glance at her and bit his lip. "I was visiting my mother's grave."

"Your mother's grave?"

"She's buried at Mounth Tower."

She'd been just a girl when Errol's mother left Edinburgh and never returned. She only remembered meeting the lady once. Errol didn't discuss her, nor did his father.

"I came to visit her grave and look over the estate my grandfather left me."

"Darleton," she whispered.

"Yes. I am now Baron of Darleton."

"That's... That's wonderful." Errol would be a close neighbor. A baron, and not just the local doctor. He'd be here forever, not just a year.

"Is it?" he said coldly. "Henderson says he has an interested buyer. I'm going to sell it."

"Sell your birthright?"

Her heart did a flip. Father wanted to buy Darleton.

"But, Errol, a buyer might tear down Mounth Tower. He might mistreat the tenants."

"My future is in London." He sat rigidly, eyes straight ahead, mouth grim.

"So that's why Henderson visited Kinmarty."

"Not entirely. He had other business here, he said."

Penelope had spent an hour closed up with him.

He'd given Ann a brief fifteen minutes during which he told her he'd informed Errol of the contractual requirement and reviewed her modest but well-placed investments. Father had been lurking and had seen her leaving the study, and, of course, had questioned her. She'd told him she was carrying a message from Penelope.

She'd become a veritable sneak since living under her father's thumb.

She drew in a deep breath. It was time she was honest with Errol.

"Ann," he said, pulling the lines and halting the horse. His arm settled around her. "You oughtn't to have traveled out here all alone."

"I was with Rolly."

"Who was no protection on the road nor from that madman I saw rushing toward the cottage."

His breath heated her lips. "Yes, you're probably right. It wasn't a sensible thing to do. But most of the grooms had gone out with the shooting party, and I didn't think to ask a footman."

"Brave girl," he whispered, and his nose touched her cheek. "But foolish."

Oh aye, she was that. She set a hand to the back of his head and pulled him into a kiss.

"Halloo," a woman called.

They jumped apart and saw two riders approaching.

"We are just in time, Urjit."

The fierce man who'd accompanied Penelope from

India leaped from his horse and Penelope slid from her saddle into his arms.

"Is that your mount tied to the back of the gig, Dr. Robillard? Yes? Well, here is what happened. Ann took the gig out to the village to… shop? Or to visit someone?" She snapped her fingers. "The vicar's daughter, remembering before she arrived that the young lady has gone off to an aunt's until Hogmanay. Dr. Robillard you were…" She tapped her chin, thinking.

"Visiting Mounth Tower," Errol said.

"Really? Well, in any case, I decided to go riding and of course, Urjit accompanied me. We encountered Ann first and then you came along. We all stopped to spy out yule logs and holly so we can return tomorrow with a wagon. Most likely all the men have returned from stalking. Ann, I believe it would be good for you to arrive at the castle with me seated beside you in the gig, instead of Dr. Robillard."

"Yes," Errol said. "Ann—"

"Don't say you're sorry," she whispered. "I certainly am not."

He grimaced. "We must talk."

A wave of guilt hit her. She'd let another chance to speak with him slip through her fingers. She'd become not just a sneak, but a coward as well.

UPON THEIR ARRIVAL AT CASTLE KINMARTY, URJIT SAW to the gig and the horses, while Errol escorted Ann and

Mrs. MacDonal into the hall where a footman took their cloaks.

Strachney strolled out of the great hall. "Where have you been, Ann?"

Errol's fists curled at the bullying tone.

Ann sent her father a tight smile. "We've been looking for a good place to collect pine boughs and holly. Oh, and a yule log."

"We'll be going out with our clippers and axes tomorrow," Mrs. MacDonal said. "I'm hoping we can get some of the energetic younger men to come with us."

Strachney harrumphed. "And you were out there looking at trees, eh, Robillard?"

"No. I was paying a call at Mounth Tower. I happened to encounter the ladies on the road. Now, I'm going to seek out the duchess."

Mrs. MacDonal put her hand on his arm. "Then you may escort us up the stairs and I'll peek into Minny's sitting room after I change."

"And I will stop there first," he said.

Errol found the duchess alone, propped on a chaise longue, a book lying open on the empty chair beside her.

"Your grace," he said, drawing nearer.

"Dr. Robillard." She smiled wanly. "How did you find Mounth Tower?"

"I suppose the duke tells you everything?"

"All but the boring bits. So will you stay on as baron and our local physician?"

"It seems I'm compelled to stay for a year, unless I can persuade my benefactor to change his mind."

"And you would wish him to do that?"

"Yes." He laughed and shook his head. "If only someone would tell me his name."

"Ask Mr. Henderson."

On the ride to Mounth Tower, he'd pointedly asked the solicitor, who'd just as firmly refused to say.

"He won't tell me. Now, your grace, how are you feeling?"

She lay back thoughtfully during his examination, and when he was finished, she sat up. "Well?" she asked. "Will it be soon?"

"You may find yourself with a Christmas baby, your grace. Unless conditions change rapidly overnight, I think it will be a few more days."

"Will you just pop your head out and tell the footman to fetch tea? Andrew left a bottle of whisky on that chest over there. Go and pour yourself some and come sit by me."

He laughed and did as he was told, seating himself in the chair and answering her questions about the state of Mounth Tower.

When the servants had brought in tea and departed, she took a sip and then set down her cup. "Mounth Tower can be restored in time," she said. "Andrew has plans for hunting at Kinmarty, and he could send his visitors over to Darleton for the fishing. You could fetch a pretty fee for that. Lovelace said that Gordon asks eight thousand pounds for the privilege of taking his salmon. I believe someone said you have salmon in your stream."

Eight thousand pounds. That couldn't be true. It was a phenomenal amount of money. "And where would I put them up, your grace?"

She pursed her lips. "They could stay here until you've refurbished enough rooms or built a lodge. I'm sure Andrew would be willing to work out an agreement with you." She took another sip of tea. "Have you seen the proposed surgery Forbes has arranged?"

"Not yet. If you don't yet need me, I'll go there tomorrow."

"It's quite cozy, I'm told. Bedrooms, a parlor and kitchen, besides the examining room and a small office. Perfect for a young doctor and his wife." She sipped again, eyeing him over the rim of her cup.

"I'm not in a position to support—"

"It will likely be a poor practice of course. You'll mostly be paid in turnips and scones. But you're a baron, with an eight-thousand-pound fishing stream, and the support of a duke."

"Who I'm told is, forgive me, poor as well."

She threw back her head and laughed. "I'm sure we could ask Penelope's help to buy medicines and whatnot."

"Thank you, but I..." He took in a breath. He wouldn't take money from a woman but saying that might be seen as an insult to the duke. "Your grace, will you just say what you want to say?"

"Yes. I suppose I ought to speak plainly. Well, Dr.

Robillard. The marquess is undoubtedly a fortune hunter. It's a pity Benedict Strachney can't marry the man himself instead of trying to woo him for his daughter. It will be a bad deal for Ann. And I've noticed the way Ann looks at you, and the way you look at her."

His heart pounded, remembering that kiss. Only Mrs. MacDonal's interruption could have torn them apart.

"You are a good match for each other. Maybe Strachney wouldn't cut her off, but if he did, I don't think our Ann is penniless. She's hinted at that from time to time. I sense her father doesn't know."

She set the cup down with a clatter and reached for his hand. "Oh, you are frowning. You're thinking I'm overstepping speaking so plainly. But you must understand that I'm a woman facing a difficult ordeal, life or—"

"No." He clamped a hand over hers. "You're going to sail through this childbirth beautifully. There'll be pain, but at the end of it, you'll hold a beautiful, perfect babe in your arms. You'll see."

Please God. He'd do his best to make certain.

"Yes. No point in being maudlin." She nodded, pushed herself up and stood. "Thank you. I'll just go and change for dinner. And Dr. Robillard, please think about what I've said."

He bowed, hiding a grimace. "I shall see you at dinner."

· · ·

AFTER THE LADIES HAD DEPARTED THE DINNER TABLE, the covers had been removed and the port had been poured, Errol moved around the table and took a seat next to Henderson.

"How did you fare the rest of your morning?" the solicitor asked.

Across the table, the golden-haired Hottentot was rattling in Strachney's ears, but the old man's beady eyes were fixed on Errol and the solicitor.

"Tell us, Robillard," Strachney barked. "What were you doing at Mounth Tower today?"

The marquess looked up. "Mounth Tower? What is Mounth Tower?"

"It is the castle of the Baron of Darleton," the duke said, with an amused glace at Errol. "A single-tower medieval edifice, I believe. Older even than Castle Kinmarty."

"It's a broken-down pile," Strachney said. "Ought to be torn down."

"Good fishing there, though, or so says Kinmarty." Warton poured himself another drink. "When may we visit and cast a line?"

"Fishing," the marquess cried. "Capital. Can you arrange that, Kinmarty? Or Strachney? He's your neighbor after all."

"Darleton's dead," Strachney said. "A recluse he was, and the staff trained to turn away all visitors. Why were you summoned, Robillard? Is there fever at Mounth Tower?"

"No," the duke said. "I'd be the first to know if there

were fever, and I otherwise trust that Dr. Robillard will maintain the confidentiality of his patients."

The other nobleman present, Cottingwith, nodded. "Kinmarty is lucky to have you, Robillard."

"There ought to be an executor or some such who can allow us access," Hottentot said. "Noble lords such as ourselves."

"Well, then, that excludes me." Warton laughed, warming to the subject. "But perhaps as a nobleman's heir, I can tag along carrying your kit. Shall we send an express to the Lord Lyon and ask him permission since the heir can't be found?"

"Damned secretive they all are," Strachney said. "I had my man checking with the Lord Lyon to find out the name of the heir. Haven't heard back from him. But Robillard, mayhap you can have a word with the steward, or butler, or housekeeper—whoever summoned you today."

Strachney had his hook placed and was pulling hard on the line.

"Capital idea," the marquess said. "One servant to another."

AN ANNOUNCEMENT

*T*he gilded prick's comment pulled Errol away from Ann's father's glare. *One servant to another?*

He wasn't a servant. He'd never been one.

He laughed, and it wasn't forced.

The marquess raised an eyebrow. "Perhaps some coins to grease the wheels, Robillard," he said. "How much do you think, gentlemen?"

Oh ho. "'Tis said…" Errol squeezed his brows together and tapped his chin, pretending to think, "that Gordon asks eight thousand pounds for the privilege of taking his salmon."

Strachney's eyes widened. The marquess's mouth dropped open and then he threw back his head and laughed. "You're having us on, Robillard. Who told you that faradiddle?"

Errol saw that the duke's lips were trembling, his eyes twinkling.

"As a matter of fact," Errol said, "I heard it from her grace, the Duchess of Kinmarty."

Henderson shifted and broke his silence. "'Tis common knowledge in these parts," he said, "Though perhaps not so well known elsewhere."

"Eight thousand," Hottentot said. "Surely we can get the baron's gamekeeper to take less than that."

"Come, Hatherot," Cottingwith said. "I've seen you drop almost that much in one night at cards."

The marquess shot the earl a cutting look, and then glanced at Strachney. "Wild oats. I was merely an earl then. Those days are long past."

"If Darleton was mine, my lord," Strachney said, "I'd let you fish there for nothing."

A look of understanding passed between the two men. If Darleton was Strachney's, if Ann was Hatherot's, fishing at Darleton would be all in the family.

Errol looked down the table at the duke, who tipped his head and raised his eyebrows.

Whether he stayed, or whether he sold, word would get out soon enough.

"As it happens…" Errol cleared his throat. "Darleton *is* mine. The castle is in no condition for visitors, but I welcome you gentlemen to ride over one day and cast your lines. At no charge." He smiled. "At least for the present."

Stunned silence reigned.

"And so," the duke raised his glass, "the Baron of Darleton has been found. Here's to you, Dr. Robillard."

"And to your excellent fishing." Cottingwith raised

his glass. "Congratulations. As I said, Kinmarty is lucky to have you."

Strachney roused out of his stupor. "But how…"

"My mother was Genevieve Callum. Mr. Henderson brought me the news. He's my grandfather's executor."

"And very secretive you were," Strachney said. "When will the Lord Lyon approve this title?"

"It is already done," Henderson said. "Now then, your grace, gentlemen, I'll excuse myself."

"Retiring so early?" the duke asked. "Or back to burning the midnight oil?"

"The latter, I fear, as I haven't brought along a clerk. I thank you for letting me set up shop in your study."

Cottingwith shifted his chair closer to Errol's and said quietly, "I hope this was good news for you, Robillard. Or should I call you Darleton?"

"Robillard is fine."

"It will be an adjustment. I inherited from a cousin a few years ago. Had a bit of sorting to do, and some worrisome quarters, but things are running smoothly now. You're lucky to have Kinmarty nearby to advise. Tell me." He paused to pour another drink, "I'd like to hear about Edinburgh. I passed through on my way north. Miss Edme Beecham says you knew her family well."

He recalled seeing Cottingwith sitting next to Edme in the breakfast room and speaking with her before dinners. Cottingwith as a suitor to Edme? He owed it to William to find out the man's intentions.

"Where is your estate?" Errol asked.

"In Kent."

So far away. Errol settled in for a long conversation nosing into this earl's character, finances, and his interests in a merchant's daughter. He wondered if Edme returned the interest.

All the while he was dimly aware that across the table the marquess and Strachney were conversing.

The marquess was wooing Ann through her father, but how did Ann feel about the man? She'd initiated that kiss today. A woman looking to marry another man wouldn't have done that.

He'd never win Strachney's heart—he wouldn't even try—but perhaps he could win Ann's.

And then what? Could he stay and make Darleton self-supporting? Could he find a buyer and convey the whole lot, title, tower, and fishing, to someone else? Could he go back to London and make his fortune there?

First things first. He drew his attention back to the earl and told him all about the Beecham's textile business, happy to see real interest and no lip curling.

THE NEXT DAY DAWNED FAIR AND, WITH THE DUCHESS proclaiming that she continued to feel well, Errol rode into the village with Forbes. The duke had convinced the marquess and Warton to visit Errol's fishing stream. Strachney had gone along—probably anxious to keep his hooks in the marquess. Henderson had already closeted himself in the study, and Cottingwith claimed a need to see to some correspondence from his man of business.

Remembering his encounter with Mrs. Gillespie the day before, Errol had fastened his smaller medical case to the horse's saddle, and a good thing it was. Before they'd even reached the surgery, they were summoned. The vicar's eldest had a boil needing lancing, a farmer had sliced a wide cut in his leg with a scythe, and the innkeeper's wife's dyspepsia had turned out to be a case of pernicious morning sickness. Already a grandmother, the poor woman had thought she was past such blessings.

Finally, after leaving the inn, Forbes led him to a stone cottage just outside the village on a well-maintained lane.

On the ground floor, a parlor sat to one side of the central entry hall, a smaller sitting room and an adjoining dining room flanking the other side of the house. Past the entry hall and stairs, another passage led to a good-sized add-on kitchen and a scullery that pumped surprisingly clear water from an underground well. Beyond that was a good-sized bothy for horses. Upstairs were four bedchambers where two men were at work repairing the plastered walls. The comfortable furnishings were piled with rolls of new wallpaper ready for hanging.

"The work will be finished soon enough," Forbes said.

Despite his plans for London, he couldn't squash a rising interest. In London, he would have shared rooms with the other members of the practice and, depending on his salary, which had never been settled, he'd likely have rented no more than a couple of rooms.

To have an entire surgery, a kitchen, home-cooked meals and perhaps a servant or two—what a luxury. The parlor would make a fine examining room, and the hall an adequate waiting room. The house would be large enough even for a man with a wife and a child or two.

Would Ann like it? She could brew her potions in that kitchen.

He shook off the thought. He was too unsettled to offer for her. Not that her father would allow a marriage. The beastly fellow would do all he could to stop one.

"What think ye, doctor? Will it do?"

It would do very well for a doctor. In fact, it was more than he'd ever imagined for a man with no money of his own starting out a new practice.

"Quite nicely," he said, and then remembered what the duchess said about the patients' ability to pay. "Depending on the rent. Will you accept payment in turnips and scones?"

Forbes laughed. "As I own the house, there's no need to fash. The rent is entirely negotiable. Though we'd like to bring in a doctor as soon as possible, we'll get the young master or miss out into the world and thriving first. When do ye reckon the babe will come?"

"From what I've seen, they come when they're good and ready."

Forbes chuckled again as he locked the door. "Off to Mounth Tower, are ye?"

"Aye. Would you like to come along and meet Busby?"

"I'm acquainted with the fellow."

"And?"

"He's honest. A bit rabbity. Might need a kick now and then. The old skinflint terrorized him. Haven't been inside the Tower for years. Aye, I think I'll join ye."

"IT'S MERE DAYS UNTIL CHRISTMAS," EDME SAID, "AND we haven't gathered nary one pine bough or holly branch. Or mistletoe."

"We must have the ribbons first," Ann said, and turned the gig onto the road that led to the village. They were off to fetch supplies for the decorations.

"Will ye kiss the marquess under the mistletoe, Ann?" Edme bumped her cousin's shoulder and giggled.

Ann thought of the kisses she'd shared with Errol and tried to imagine the marquess pressing his lips to hers. She shuddered. "Kissing a marquess. Why does that not excite me? But what about you and Lord Cottingwith?"

Color rose in her cousin's face and tinted her frown pink. "Is he courting me? I don't think so. I think he's just shy and he finds me safe to talk to." Edme leaned forward and pointed. "Oh, look over there."

On the distant road a bedraggled figure wrapped in

a tartan carried a burden. Ann slapped the ribbons and the horse picked up its pace, and then slowed to a stop alongside the woman who'd shrunk to the side of the road.

"Maggie," she shouted. "What's happened?"

"Thought ye was runnin' us over," she cried in a shaky voice. "'Tis Rolly."

"Me leg," the boy said. Silent tears streamed down the dirty little face, pink from the drying blood. Both legs of the baggy trousers were dark with dirt, but one was a mud red.

Ann handed the ribbons to Edme and jumped down. "Is it broken?"

"Think so," Maggie said.

Errol had left the castle that morning to visit the village. Would he still be there? "We've almost reached the village," Ann said. "We'll put Rolly in the box on your lap, Maggie, go to the inn, and then send someone to find Dr. Robillard."

"He's at the new surgery," Maggie said. "Not more than a mile."

Her heart pounded harder. If Errol had a surgery, maybe he planned to stay.

"Then let's get Rolly up."

Edme handed down her cloak. "Cushion him with this," she said.

He screamed as they transferred him, but settled on his mother's lap and the makeshift cushion. With Ann's cloak covering him, they crawled down the lane following Maggie's directions.

At the small cottage they found Errol and Forbes just getting ready to mount.

ERROL TOOK ONE LOOK AT MAGGIE'S MOTTLED, BRUISED, face, and swallowed his anger.

"Rolly is hurt," Ann called, jumping down from the bench. "His leg might be broken."

He hurried to the box and peeled back the blue fur-lined mantle he recognized as Ann's. Next to him, Ann shivered, and he felt the heat of her breath as he gingerly probed the swelling limb. "Forbes, have your workmen fetch a board or small table."

Forbes ran in and swiftly returned with the two workmen carrying a door, and Ann helped transfer the child onto the flat surface.

Inside, they carried the boy to the dining table and set the board upon it. Bodies pressed all around.

He heard Ann's quiet murmurs. The workmen moved off, and Edme went through the door to the kitchen.

"What's happened here, Mrs. Gillespie?" Errol asked.

Her gaze shifted away. "He fell."

The boy—Rolly, Ann had called him—looked to be not more than six years old. His gaze followed his mother.

"Maggie," Forbes said, his voice gentle. "What did that man of yours do this time?"

Her lip jutted out. "'twere an accident. Can ye help him, please, doctor? Please help him."

He let Forbes deal with the woman, while he opened the lad's worn jacket. The scrawny creature was skin and bones. He'd been crying, but he wasn't doing so now. He looked like he was going into shock. "I'm Dr. Robillard. Do you remember me, Rolly?"

"Aye," he said on a faint breath.

The red blotches on his chest would turn purple later but the boy's ribs seemed intact. The blood seeping through that trouser leg meant Ann had probably had the right of it. That had to come first before checking further for broken ribs or damaged internal organs.

Ann handed him a pair of scissors. "I have Edme fetching hot water. Forbes, are there any clean flannels or towels anywhere?"

"Aye. Had the household linens stocked already upstairs in case the doctor wanted to stay."

Rolly's eyes fluttered and closed, and his mother began sobbing.

"Now there, Maggie," Ann said. "You must cease your crying. It will only make this harder for Rolly. Go into the kitchen and help Edme."

Errol took out his scissors and began snipping the trouser leg.

Maggie shrieked. "Those be his only breeches—"

"Go now, lass." Forbes had returned bearing a stack of towels, and there was steel in his command. Her tearful moans retreated, and he heard the door creak shut.

One of the workmen came in carrying a load of wood. "We'll get this fire going, as well," Forbes said.

"Thank you." In truth, Errol had ceased feeling the chill the moment he'd seen the lump under the coarse cloth.

Carefully he snipped, an inch at a time, lifting the cloth gingerly, laying the leg bare.

A moan escaped the pinched little mouth, and Ann rested her hand on the boy's head.

Errol probed gently and let out a breath, relieved that no bone poked through. He snipped an inch further and found a ragged gash.

He touched the leg again, and the boy blinked, a bit of the shock clearing. The pain would soon surface again, and this time in spades.

"Your leg bone is broken, young Rolly. And you've a cut here. I wonder how that happened?"

"Splinters," Forbes muttered.

"T' chair broke," Rolly whispered.

He'd best pull those out before they festered. "Light that lamp, Forbes and move it closer. I think you are a very brave lad, and I will ask you to be a bit braver. Will you do that for me?"

He covered the wound with a cloth and probed again, ever so gently. Rolly jerked, but Ann was there, quietly steadying the boy.

"Very good, Rolly. I believe you have a clean break here." He looked up into Ann's eyes.

"I'll go check on that hot water," she said.

"No, I'll go," Forbes said.

"And Forbes, find us a couple of boards for a splint."

Ann produced a handkerchief and began wiping the boy's damp cheeks. "Perhaps a wee drop of the laudanum, doctor?" She looked around. "And some whisky to clean the wound?"

"Forbes keeps a bottle in the cabinet across the hall. There's laudanum in my bag." He cursed quietly. "It's on my horse."

Ann stepped away a moment and returned carrying his bag. "Forbes had his man bring it in. Ah, here's Edme with hot water."

She sent her cousin out again to fetch a cup of cool water and then hurried out and returned with Forbes's whisky.

"Water," Edme said handing over a cup. "I'll fetch the basin for you, Dr. Robillard."

"We'll start with the tiniest drop." Errol handed Ann a vial and watched as she carefully doled out the dose and raised the boy's head.

"Rolly," she said, "This medicine will make the pain easier."

The boy turned his head away, and she made soothing sounds. "Here, lad, don't ye remember when ye had the fever last year? The tisane I gave ye made ye better, didn't it? This will help ease the pain so the doctor can make your leg better."

Errol went to the side table and washed, glancing back. Ann was cradling Rolly's head as he took tiny sips.

He uncorked the bottle of whisky and took a whiff of the heady brew. He poured it onto his hands and rubbed them together. Then he retrieved a fresh cloth, dampened it with the whisky, and began cleaning around the open wound, his tweezers at the ready as he waited for the laudanum to relax the boy.

The blood was drying, and the fresh oozing had slowed by the time he began drawing out slivers of wood.

"And how are those wee lambs born last spring," Ann asked.

Rolly mumbled, and she chattered on, asking him about the sheep and the dog he'd befriended to help him tend them.

Ann wasn't normally a chatterer, was she? Perhaps he hadn't noticed before.

Her cheerfulness seemed to sooth the boy, and it was easing the rattling inside him. Setting a bone could be tricky and, in one as young as this, a bad job might mean a lifetime of pain or a permanent limp.

Maggie arrived with more hot water, and Forbes came carrying a handful of boards of different sizes.

The boy's eyes had grown heavy, but when he spotted his mother he stirred and began sobbing.

"Miss Beecham," Forbes said, "Can ye take the gig and run to the inn for a basket of food? Maggie, ye go with her and help her carry."

"Mr. Forbes and I will look after Rolly while the doctor fixes his leg," Ann said.

"My place is with—"

Rolly squirmed.

"Go," Errol said. "Help her out, Forbes, and then come back."

"Come along, Maggie," Edme said.

"There now." Ann stroked the boy's head. "All will

be well. You needn't be troubled. Dr. Robillard is a kind man and a good doctor. Why, the duke himself brought him here to deliver the duchess's baby. He'll fix it so you'll be running faster than ever after the wee ones at lambing time."

She sent him a long look and smiled.

His heart squeezed. She was the woman for him, if he could but find a way.

"Thank you," he said.

When they looked down, Rolly's eyes were fluttering shut.

"Now," he said. "Hold him well, Ann."

It was full dark when they crept up to Kinmarty Castle in the duke's carriage. Errol had deemed it impossible to return the boy to the Gillespie cottage, so Forbes had ridden to Kinmarty and fetched the carriage back. The crofter's wife and son would spend the night there.

Ann hadn't had a moment's chance to speak freely to Errol that afternoon, and she saw immediately that she wouldn't have a chance that evening. Her father scowled from the doorway as two footmen under Errol's direction transferred the board carrying Rolly into the castle, his mother following in his wake.

Another footman helped Edme descend, and Ann followed.

"What's the meaning of this, Kinmarty?" Father asked the duke, who was shaking Errol's hand.

"Forbes said the inn is no place for this injured

child," the duke said, "and now that I see him, I agree. Devil of an afternoon, eh, Robillard? Strachney, I congratulate you on your daughter's good sense. You did well, Miss Strachney, Forbes said. You as well, Miss Beecham."

"The hard job was Dr. Robillard's," Ann said. "I've never seen a bone set."

Errol smiled, looking terribly tired. "And I've never seen a terrified child persuaded to take medicine so easily."

Edme laughed. "She had a great deal of practice on my little brothers."

"We've delayed dinner for you," the duke said. "But as you all look done in after this day, we can send trays up to your rooms if you'd prefer."

"Nonsense," Strachney said. "Ann will go and change for dinner."

Edme scoffed and quickly turned it into a cough. "Well, if you go, I go, cousin."

"Please go ahead without me," Errol said. "I'll see my patient settled in and then I'll check on the duchess before she retires."

Ann watched the housekeeper lead Errol and his party up the stairs.

Tomorrow. Tomorrow she would have a chance to speak with him.

THE NEXT MORNING, SHE AND EDME WERE THE FIRST to arrive at the breakfast room. Cottingwith appeared, his eyes drooping until he saw Edme. He claimed a seat next to her and went to fill her a plate.

"Did the card game run late?" Ann took the plate prepared by the footman on duty.

"Until the wee hours, I believe. I left before I lost my estate." He smiled. "That was a joke. I never play for high stakes."

But Warton and Hatherot did. "Did Father play?"

"Yes, and he was holding his own. The duke wisely begged off. Ah." He looked up. "Robillard, how are your patients today?"

Errol's smile sent a shiver of hope through her. He was unaccountably cheerful, like the old Errol she'd once known. "Rolly is on the mend, and the duchess is not in labor." He went to the sideboard and then took the seat next to her.

"The others are sleeping late?" Edme asked. "No shooting for you today?"

"No shooting, and no fishing," Cottingwith said. "What say we try a different sort of hunt? I've heard you ladies discussing gathering pine boughs."

"And mistletoe," Errol said. "You mustn't forget that." He passed her a dish of preserves and his fingers brushed hers.

Ann's heart leapt in her chest and pounded. Would she be able to steal a moment alone with him? Would he hate her forever when she told him the truth? Or could he possibly care for her?

"Mistletoe is very important," Edme said. "I think we should hurry through breakfast and leave the slugabeds to sleep late."

"Excellent idea. What do you think, Dr. Robillard?"

"By all means. The sooner we go, the sooner I'll be able to get back and check on young Rolly's leg. What say you, Ann?"

She couldn't eat another bite, not with Errol's braw presence next to her, and the promise of being alone with him. Almost alone. "I'll get my warm things and ask the butler if he can spare a footman to help carry boughs."

THE FOOTMAN PROVED INVALUABLE AT DIRECTING THEM to patches of evergreen trees and holly. The fellow had also had the presence of mind to fetch a groom who brought shears and a donkey to carry their burdens. Soon the paniers were almost filled.

"'Tis an old oak over that next rise," said the footman. "Mayhap ye'll find some mistletoe there."

Cottingwith offered his arm. "Let's go, Miss Beecham." Edme giggled and the two headed off.

"Catch up, Ann," Edme called over her shoulder.

Errol watched them leave and turned to Ann. Her cheeks had grown rosy in the cold. They'd been laughing before, but something had changed, and the look on her face was serious, almost apprehensive.

"What's wrong?" he asked.

She opened her mouth, but a rustling noise made them turn before she could reply.

"Good morning." Mrs. MacDonal came from a side path on the arm of her Indian manservant, Urjit. "You went out without us, I see. Where is Edme? I believe I'm meant to be chaperoning you girls."

The Indian servant sent Mrs. MacDonal a wry look, and she chuckled.

Errol almost joined in the laughter. Though gray threaded Urjit's beard, he was not old, at least not too old for Mrs. MacDonal. There was an aura of... deep friendship there.

"She and Cottingwith are hunting mistletoe," he said pointing in the direction the others had gone. "We'll be right behind you."

ANN WATCHED AS URJIT LIFTED THE LADY OVER A PATCH of rocky ground and then continue on, holding her hand fast to his arm.

"Well," he said, studying the departing couple. "Such a friendship wouldn't go over well with society, which perhaps is why she keeps to the Highlands," he mused.

"I believe it may be something deeper than friendship. And I won't gossip about someone who's been quite kind to me."

He turned a warm gaze on her, set down his shears, and took both her hands in his. "You misunderstand. I'm wondering if you and I might ever share that sort of intimacy? You're wealthy now. I'm not, but I intend to work hard."

Her heart twisted again. She must just pluck up her nerve and tell him the truth. After that, there'd be no need to make plans.

Instead, she blurted, "Errol, you and I, we are not in

that situation. We are both Scottish citizens. Both of the middling classes, despite father's wealth. Well, and until your grandfather died leaving you the barony. You outrank me, but otherwise we are perfectly matched."

"Ann, do you care for me? I'm not at all sure I'll be able to support you. But I could send for you, once I get my practice established in London."

"London? You don't like it here?"

"I do, but... I believe I should stick to my plan. Henderson has an interested buyer for Darleton. I just need to find the benefactor and ask to work out a repayment plan."

FOOTSTEPS CRUNCHED AND ERROL TURNED, STILL holding her hands. Strachney stood in the middle of the path, a nasty smile curling through his ruddy layers of fat.

A SECRET REVEALED

"There's no need to search further, Robillard. You can simply ask your benefactor directly. Isn't that right, daughter?"

Ann colored deeply, her lips thinning and her jaw hardening. "Go away, Father," she said, steel in her voice.

"You'll not speak to me that way. I've seen Henderson's papers. I don't know how you obtained the money, but I'll see that it's transferred to me."

Tears flooded her eyes and stayed there, her face mottling with suppressed anger. "I wasn't a minor when the money came to me, and I'm not now. And I wish to speak with Errol alone. Go away."

And then he knew.

His heart sank, taking the life blood with it. Ann had an inheritance. She'd paid for his schooling. She was his benefactor, and she had demanded he come to the Highlands.

Damn and blast it all. She'd been scheming.

"You'll not talk to me that way." Strachney took a step toward her, and Errol moved in between them.

He'd been duped, made a fool of by this wee slip of a girl. Still, he wouldn't stand for her father's bullying. Though in her own quiet way, she was as much of a bully as her father.

"Move out of my way, Robillard."

Errol clenched his fists. He'd tossed more than one drunken brute out of his father's common room.

"Not in your present state of mind, Strachney."

"I said move," Strachney shouted, and his fist shot out.

Errol dodged and gripped the man's wrist, yanking him around. Behind him, Ann gasped, and a woman shouted.

Urjit appeared and grasped Strachney's other arm.

"What is going on?" Mrs. MacDonal asked. "Are you quite all right, Dr. Robillard?"

Strachney spluttered, his gaze raking over the two men holding him.

Robillard released him. "I'm fine. And now I must check on the duchess. Will you kindly escort Ann back to the castle?"

ANN GULPED BACK TEARS, WATCHING HIS PROUD BACK AS he strode down the path, anger and pain warring in her.

"Dear Ann, are you alright?" The older lady wrapped an arm around Ann and cast her father a hard gaze.

"Be off with you, Mrs. MacDonal," he said. "This is a matter between me and my daughter."

Penelope scoffed. "Oh? It appeared to be a matter between you and Dr. Robillard. Or was Dr. Robillard interceding in Ann's behalf? Were you planning to use that fist on your daughter? In the Duke of Kinmarty's lands?"

Father's mouth firmed, but he had enough sense to pull back. He loved to brag about his money and his influence, but news of such vulgarity—striking his daughter or the duke's physician—would travel fast.

He was, after all, a guest in the home of a duke, a duke who had resources outside of the Strachney fortune.

Plus, there were influential noblemen visiting.

"I've been surprised you've not availed yourself much of the hunting, Strachney," Mrs. MacDonal said. "If you don't wish to hunt, or if your business is so pressing as to keep you from it, perhaps you may want to return to Glenthistle. Ann, of course, will stay here. The duchess appreciates her help." She smiled at Urjit and linked arms with Ann. "Urjit, will you escort us to the castle? You may see your daughter at dinner, Strachney" she said. "If you decide to remain."

Mrs. MacDonal pulled her along, while Urjit followed, guarding them against Father's ire.

"Would you like to share what that was about?" the lady whispered.

Tears welled and threatened to brim over. "I have money of my own, Mrs. MacDonal. Not a great deal, but enough that I was able to pay Errol's university fees."

"Foolish men and their pride," she muttered.

ERROL FOUND THE DUKE SEATED ON THE BED, WHILE HIS wife nibbled her breakfast from a tray, and Ravi and Arun perched on either side of her helping themselves to buttered scones.

The boys shouted greetings, and the duke beamed at him, so obviously happy, he swallowed his own anger and smiled back.

"We've come to an agreement," the duke said. "If the child is a boy, we're calling him Evan, after my late brother."

"Our papa," Arun said.

"A good name, your grace. And if it's a girl?"

"We're still negotiating that," the duchess said, with a wry smile. "Because, of course, it must be a boy.

"Lovelace will be godfather," the duke said.

"Yes, and we've thought to ask Ann to stand as godmother along with Penelope."

Would the duchess never cease pushing Ann on him?

He mustered his courtesy. "That is a great honor." If the child was a boy, Ann would be godmother to a future duke. Strachney would be thrilled.

"She is excellent with these two mischievous boys," the duchess said ruffling Arun's hair, "and a good nurse. In different circumstances, I wonder if she would have liked to be a midwife."

Knowing Ann, she'd prefer to push her way into a profession as an apothecary, or perhaps even a surgeon.

"Strachney would never allow that." The duke stood, dropped a kiss on his wife's forehead and took her tray away. "But you are here to examine my lady, I presume, not talk about Ann."

"Quite right, sir."

"Come along, boys," the duke said. "Back to the nursery. One game of dominoes."

They leapt off the bed and departed, wheedling the duke for more than one game. The duke paused at the door. "Join me in the library after, Robillard," he said.

ALL SEEMED WELL WITH THE DUCHESS AND HE LEFT HER in the care of her maid.

He met the duke on the landing, his neckcloth askew.

"Well met," the duke said. "The curate appeared for the boys' lessons, and so I escaped after one game. Come along. The others are still abed, I presume, and won't bother us."

Once there, he rang for tea and seated himself near the fire, indicating the chair across from him.

One didn't refuse tea with an affable duke... and yet, would this interminable morning never end?

"Bad business with the poor lad. How is he?" Kinmarty asked.

"When I saw him early this morning he was diving into his porridge. No fever. Time will tell how well the leg mends. A neighbor promised to tend their chickens and their few sheep, but he and his mother are anxious to get home and see to them themselves. It's likely we can send him home in a few days with some crutches if he'll be safe there. Have you heard aught from Forbes about his father?"

"Packed a kit and left for a cousin's house before he and the vicar could reach his cottage." He paused and drummed the desktop. "He's a Darleton tenant, I understand."

His neckcloth suddenly felt too tight. "Aye, your grace." The boy was, technically, his own responsibility, a burden he didn't want. "Do you... do you have any advice to offer on the best way to deal with the father?"

"Outside of running him to ground and beating the pulp out of him?"

Errol had considered that notion and rejected it as a bit too direct as the first approach. Violence might be all the dastard would understand, yet he might turn it onto his wife and son once Errol left.

The duke set a booted foot on the fireplace fender. "I might suggest the Justice of the Peace but..." The library door opened, drawing his attention. "Ah, here is Henderson. Perhaps we should ask him. Do you have time for a chat, Henderson, or... I see that you're frowning. What's afoot?"

Henderson bowed and pulled over a chair. "I'm at your service, your grace, at least through tomorrow, and then I plan to leave for Inverness the day after. But yes, while I hesitate to make assumptions or point fingers, someone has been in my files."

Errol's chest tightened. The duke sat up.

"Is anything missing?" the duke asked.

"No, only disarranged. And I did see one of the guests in the corridor outside the study as I came around the corner."

"I shall give you a key," the duke said. "I ought to have done so already. If you would like to tell me the name of the guest, I'll have a word with him."

"It was Strachney," Errol said. "Searching out Ann's business." His face heated but it was a cold rage building within him. "He encountered us in the woods and told us as much. He became belligerent with Ann. The fool actually took a swing at me."

The duke pressed his lips together and shook his head. "I was about to say, Robillard, that I might suggest having the Justice of the Peace see to your tenant, Gillespie, but Strachney has set himself up in that role."

Gillespie ought to be horse-whipped, but Strachney might have the man hanged on a whim. "I wouldn't turn any man over to Strachney," Errol said.

"I heard about the poor lad," Henderson said. "He has a right to discipline his son, but he'll likely claim the injury was an accident."

"He'd just beat his wife the day before," Errol said glumly. Husbands had a right to do that as well.

"Before you send the lad back, we'll go together and search for Gillespie," the duke said, "and put the fear of God into him."

As concerned as he was for Maggie and Rolly—and he was, despite wanting to sell Darleton—he was even more concerned for Ann. She'd reached her majority, but who was to keep her father from beating her. Or, a husband from doing so, if the old man married her off to a fortune hunter for a title.

Henderson cleared his throat. "Dr. Robillard, I've just heard from a colleague and learned the name of the prospective buyer for Darleton. It's Benedict Strachney."

"Damnation," he muttered. "Beg pardon, your grace, Mr. Henderson."

"And may I add, given the chance to develop sport fishing commercially at Darleton, his offer is far below value."

"You could make an outrageous counteroffer if you really don't want to sell to him," the duke said. "It's a true fact Strachney would have no problem handling Gillespie. He'd pack him, his family, and all the neighbors off to the antipodes and give the land over to sheep farms. He would have done that at Glenthistle, but he only has a lease on the manor house."

"Why a lease?" Errol asked. "Why didn't he look elsewhere and buy... ah."

A grimace crossed the duke's face. "I imagine he decided proximity to an unmarried duke would give him a leg up on getting his daughter well-married. Odd that, since my brother was heir. Perhaps he was wagering that Evan wouldn't survive India." His fist came down on the chair arm. "Or maybe he'd learned Darleton was dying and had no heir. Man's obsessed with titles. If you sell him Darleton, he'll be a Scottish baron."

"It's not a peerage title," Henderson said. "But I suppose if his daughter becomes a marchioness, it might give him more prestige than presenting himself as a mere mister."

Errol's heart sank. Everyone assumed Ann would marry this Hottentot fellow.

She didn't want the marquess, but it would serve her right, the manipulative, conniving... No, that was unjust. She'd been deceptive because she'd had to be. Elsewise, he'd have never taken her money.

His hands fisted in his lap. Ann to be sold off for a title. His mother's grave under the care of a bully—if he sold the estate.

He could ask Henderson to seek out other buyers. Or... he hadn't fully looked at the possibility of trying to run Darleton from his new position in London. Perhaps the duke would allow Forbes to look in on Busby while Errol was away.

That, of course, would require Ann releasing him from the contract. But then she'd be left in the clutches of her father and the marquess.

He swiped a hand through his hair. He had a patient needing tending, and he needed to talk to Ann. "If you'll excuse me, your grace, Mr. Henderson, I need to check on Rolly now, but Mr. Henderson, I'd like to have a few moments of your time later."

THE DUKE SOUGHT HIM OUT AGAIN AFTER HIS VISIT TO Rolly.

"Henderson is ensconced with Penelope," he said.

"Fil has put Ann to work on a christening gown. Shall we go visit some of the tenants? We may just get lucky and encounter Gillespie. We've some cottages where sickness seems more prevalent. We've been working on improving the wells and making sure the families have enough food. I'd like to hear what other recommendations you might have."

The duke was poking at an interest of his—contagious diseases caused by poor sanitation. If he stayed, he might be able to do some good.

His heart thudded. But how would he live? The duke had no obligation to pay him a salary. Unless he wanted to discuss the matter with his benefactor—and he didn't and wouldn't—he'd have to get his living from the pennies and groats the poor crofters could offer.

He went to get his medical bag, frustration eating at him.

THE NEXT DAY, ERROL FOUND HIMSELF BACK IN THE cottage that housed the new surgery. The drapers and painters had finished the upstairs, and every bedroom had a respectable bed and clothes press.

Respectable, but not new, except for the bed ropes and straw-filled mattresses. The antique furniture likely had come from Kinmarty Castle's attics, but it had been cleaned of dust and cobwebs, and polished.

The quest for Gillespie had been unsuccessful. After dinner the night before, he'd had an unfruitful meeting with Henderson. In his role as executor of his grandfather's estate, he'd offered guidance. But to represent Errol further in a sale of the property and conveyance of the title—well, there would be costs. Like any good doctor, a solicitor wouldn't work for free.

He'd had no chance to speak with Ann. Seated next to Mr. Warton, she'd been subdued, allowing the rattlepate Warton to chatter away with the merry marquess across from them. When the gentlemen joined the ladies in the drawing room, Ann was nowhere to be found. The duchess had whisked her away.

Though he and the duke hadn't found Gillespie, they'd encountered a whole host of medical complaints, so many that he'd promised to return. Soon enough, he was downstairs in the examining room treating small wounds, aching backs, and a plethora of chilblains.

He'd started his own fires, fetched his own water from the well, and his own back was aching by the time he'd cleared the room.

He was sorting his medical bag, preparing to visit the inn for the sake of his gnawing stomach when he heard the door open again.

"Can you come back?" he called. "I'm just going to fetch an ale."

"I've brought you a basket," a breathless voice said.

Ann stood, all but hidden by the blue mantle that dipped down to her eyebrows and covered everything down to her gloved hands and the large basket draped with a white cloth.

He crossed to the door in two strides and took the heavy thing. She pushed her hood back and he could see that her cheeks and nose were bright red from the cold.

"Good God, did you walk from the castle?"

"It's not far."

He glanced out the window. He hadn't noticed the sky darkening. A gust of wind blew the door open, and he went to close and latch it.

The weather was changing. If he wasn't mistaken, they'd have snow for Christmas. Or worse, icy sleet that would keep him penned up in the Highlands until the next thaw.

"Cook made meat pies for you," she said. "And there's some wine and a jug of ale. I've brought a tin of tea, some bread, butter, and biscuits and dried fruit as well." She eyed the door and then shot him a challenging glare. "I should like to stay and have tea with you before I return."

He didn't know whether to glare back or laugh at her bossiness, so part and parcel of her high-handedness. Before he could decide, her gaze dropped, long lashes hiding what she was feeling, lashes beaded with moisture—from the walk in the cold or were those tears?

She lifted her chin and said in a haughty voice. "Very well. Give me the b-basket..." She cleared her throat. "And I'll put away the food while you go to the inn." Her hand shot out, her lower lip jutted, and she tugged at the handle.

Now he did laugh, and that set her eyes to flashing.

"Blast you and your arrogant pride, Errol." She let go of the handle and with more speed than he could have imagined, turned, jerked the door open and ran out.

"ANN, WAIT."

She heard footsteps behind her, and she yanked her skirts higher and ran faster. The muddy lane was slickening with the freeze, and it was bloody cold, the mist prickling like fine shards of glass.

Bloody Errol. The basket had been merely an excuse; she'd called on him for a chance to speak in private. To release him from any commitment. To beg him to not sell Glenthistle to her father. To explain.

Now... forget him. She'd direct Henderson to send him a letter.

The clomping behind her grew louder. Chest aching, she picked up her pace. A little further and she'd be on the high street, and he wasn't likely to chase her there.

A hand clamped over her arm. "Ann, stop."

She tried to yank out of his grasp, her boots skidded, and they both went down.

Just like the day in her uncle's garden, only this time, Errol was on top of her.

"Get off, you oaf." She shoved at his shoulder.

He stared down at her, that same expression of wonder she'd seen that day, right before he—

His lips touched hers, and a hand slid under and lifted her head.

Oh. Heat sizzled through her. His lips pressed and

moved, and his tongue touched hers, tender, and then more firmly, he took control, addling her brains, sending desire coursing through her and pooling in a warm muddle of something she'd never felt and couldn't describe.

"Ann," he murmured into her ear, directing his kisses to her neck. "Forgive me, Ann. I oughtn't to have laughed."

Laughing was the least of their problems. With her heart pounding, and his lips evoking waves of pleasure in her, it was hard to think straight.

Why had she come? Oh yes, to talk to him.

She didn't want to talk. She wanted to kiss him, and more, to carry the kissing through to the logical conclusion.

To experience lovemaking before being forced into a loveless marriage.

The duchess had described the new surgery building in detail. The cottage had four bedchambers.

"Errol," she said before she could lose her nerve. "Let's go inside where it's warmer."

He raised his head with a stunned look, rolled off her, and helped her to her feet. "I beg your pardon, Ann." His expression altered, falling back into polite neutrality. "You must think me a beast."

She shook some of the dirt from her cloak. "Why would I? I kissed you back."

"Come," he said. He took her arm and hurried her toward the cottage. "We'll eat some of those meat pies. But why are you really here? Does the duchess need me?"

"No, not yet. I wanted to talk, to explain." She stopped him before the door and took in a shaky breath. "I paid your university fees because I wanted to help you, and I had the means to do so, and you... you deserved the help, in spite of the fact that you're... you were such an *arse*." Now that the words were coming, she had to get them all out, and let him reject her if he would. She could turn and go back down the road to the castle. "I meant to tell you myself. I've been trying. And I had no idea you'd found a position in London. And I came today to tell you, you must accept it. You must go. You must follow your dream."

The look he turned on her was thunderous. His damnable pride again. He'd fuss and insist on paying her back, but leave he would, that was certain. The kisses had meant nothing compared to his ambition.

Never mind. She swallowed sudden moisture and went on. "I never meant to hurt you. I lo..."

"Dr. Robillard." A horseman was flying up the lane, too fast. It was Will, one of the grooms from Kinmarty. He jumped from the saddle. "Ye're needed at t'castle, Dr. Robillard."

A MOST DIFFICULT PATIENT

"*I*s the duchess—"

He shook his head and fumbled his cap, his face pinched and white. "Been an accident. With a gun."

"What was the injury?" Errol asked.

"A chest wound. A gun exploded. Some shrapnel, some powder burns."

"Right," he said. "I have some medical supplies at the castle. I'll have what I need there to get started. My horse is in back. I'll take yours. Fetch a gig for Miss Strachney from the inn and bring her and my medical bag."

Will crouched to give him a leg up.

She turned to go back inside, but a sudden premonition had her call over her shoulder. "Who was injured?"

· · ·

WILL PRESSED HIS LIPS TOGETHER AND SHOT ANN A pitying look. She came and stood next to the groom, her face going paler.

"Out with it," Errol said, more harshly than he meant to.

"'Twas Mr. Strachney, sir."

"Ann," he said. "You're coming with me. Will, toss her up here. Gather my medical kit and bring it along as soon as you're able."

He'd never had the chance to be much of a horseman, and he prayed he could keep his seat and not lose Ann, seated palfrey style in front of him. Clutching her to him, he spurred the poor beast, fighting the trembling in his heart. Benedict Strachney was a brute of a father set on ruining his daughter's life, and the lives of the Darleton tenants if he was able. Nevertheless, he'd taken an oath and he'd do all that he could to save the reprobate.

Damn, damn, damn.

"'Twas his blasted new gun, I'll warrant," she said. "He'd been anxious to show it off to the lords coming here, but the action was off, and he'd had one of his men fiddling with it."

He tightened his hold. "We'll patch him up, Ann." Her skirts billowed in the wind, and her soft feminine scent filled him with confidence. She belonged in his arms.

She looked back at him, and her hood slipped, and he saw the worry there. Mayhap she loved the crusty old man.

"I ought to have asked how bad it is," she said. "We

had a local man last year shot accidentally by the duke's gamekeeper. I picked out buckshot for hours, and the poor man's face will be forever scarred."

"*You* picked it out? Not one of the men? The apothecary, or barber, or someone?"

"The apothecary is too fond of his whisky to be always steady of hand, and the barber is far too ham-handed for a bullet extraction. They called me, and I helped them."

"Did your father know what you were about?"

"He'd gone up to Edinburgh on business."

"Does he know that you see to the medical needs of the people?"

He held his breath, waiting to see if she would deny it.

"Visiting the poor is a great lady's occupation, isn't it?"

She would have found a way to convince her father of that.

"I'm going to do all I can to save him, Ann."

"You couldn't do any less and be you, Errol."

ANN'S HEART RACED AS THE DUKE HIMSELF ESCORTED them to the bedchamber where they'd carried her father.

Errol entered, but the duke stopped her outside in the corridor. "Ann," he said. "Might you not want to wait in the parlor? Filomena will join you. He may not want you to see him like this."

"He is conscious?"

"Yes, and in great pain. His man and the butler are with him, and one of the footmen."

She shook her head. "I must go in. He'll be beastly to Errol."

"He's likely to be beastly to you as well."

She pressed a hand to her forehead. "So be it. I won't let Errol go through this alone. It's my fault he's here." She pushed past the duke, her gaze sweeping the chamber. Father's brushes and shaving kit lay on a dressing table, and a footman was picking up discarded clothes.

Errol's medical bag sat on the table near the bed, open to display his essential tools and medicines. Her father's stocking-clad feet stretched at the end of the bed. She moved closer.

His coats and shirt had been stripped away. She'd never seen her father's bulky paunch.

Father's valet stood holding a linen compress gingerly to the broad chest, as each breath came in a labored wheeze. The butler stood at his other side.

Ann pressed a hand to her own chest. She'd been stripped of all hope today, knowing that Errol would take her up on her offer to release him from a year's commitment, that he would choose to leave Kinmarty, to leave her, knowing she would either have to marry against her wishes to a man of her father's choice, or leave her home and her father and somehow make her own way.

But she'd never wished for her father to die. His death wouldn't make her life easier; it would only be more fraught with grief and guilt.

Errol approached the bed and signaled the servant to move away. When he lifted away the bandage, he blinked, and then his gaze settled back into an analytical frown.

"Strachney," he said. "Can you hear me?"

"Get your filthy hands off me." Strachney smacked at Errol's hand, and squealed, from the pain of the movement or the force of the men holding him back she wasn't sure.

"Right, then." Errol went to the washstand and returned.

"Will this work?" Ann had a probe ready for him.

"Thank you." His gaze sparked warmth within her, the two simple words giving her foolish hope.

"Father," she said, "lie as still as you possibly can while the doctor examines you."

"Damn you, girl. I did it all for you and you'd throw it away on this… this… *Ow.* You're hurting me."

A gash traced from the top of his chest to the skin of the stomach, the fleshy layers oozing blood. Errol poked gently around the edges. "You've powder burns on your shoulders and upper chest. But here… tweezers, Ann, please."

She fetched him the instrument and watched as he pulled out a sliver of wood, making her father howl and hurl curses so foul she winced. For all of his airs, her father cursed like the lowest of scallywags.

But he'd pulled himself up, hadn't he? Mother's family had not approved of him as a husband. That was why her godmother, her mother's lifelong friend, made sure her inheritance would not be under his control.

"Ann." Errol's mouth firmed. "Will you not wait outside. I'd not have you subjected to this abuse."

"Abuse?" Strachney cried. "That drunken apothecary could do the job better. This one's poking harder on purpose."

"*Father*. Errol is doing his best. If he doesn't remove the bits and pieces from the wound they'll fester."

Father swore a vile oath about Errol's parentage.

The duke took her hand and rubbed it between his own. "Men don't handle pain well, Ann. Your father is worse than most. With so much rot pouring from your mouth, Strachney, the wound may fester anyway."

"I'll do my very best to save you," Errol said. "Though God knows why I should."

As he worked, her father's voice grew hoarser with each bellow and insult. She tried to shut them out, as Errol seemed able to do, but she found herself giving into the duke's gentle tugging, edging her away from the bed, until another arm came around her shoulder.

"Come into my parlor," Mrs. MacDonal said. "You may cry on my shoulder if you wish."

She glanced back at Errol and found him watching her. Pain flashed briefly in his dark eyes, quickly shuttered. He nodded and went back to his work, as if nothing had happened.

She straightened her shoulders and linked arms with Mrs. MacDonal. "I have no intentions of weeping."

"Not even out of anger?"

"Perhaps that. But I'll go and drink tea and wait to hear whether my father dies today."

"Or to see whether Errol kills him or not?"

"I'd kill them both if I was that sort of woman."

A servant arrived with the tea tray, and they waited until he left.

"If he dies, will you stay at Glenthistle?"

"I don't know." Tears sprang to her eyes, unbidden, as she thought about living in the great house near Kinmarty, all alone. Her aunt wouldn't join her; she wouldn't want to leave Edinburgh where her sons ran the business and she cared for her younger children.

But how could she leave the tenants, and the local people? They needed her.

She'd dreamed of a year, and maybe more, in the Highlands with Errol. Perhaps working side-by-side. Wondering if maybe someday, he could care for her.

Oh, his kisses proved he cared for her. He just wouldn't stay.

If her father lived, she could marry the marquess, but that way lay even deeper loneliness. If Father died, she wouldn't have to marry anyone.

Oh, but she didn't care about being an heiress.

"I would like to stay, but to live at Glenthistle all alone?" She shuddered.

"And what of Errol."

She shook her head. "I released him from his commitment today."

"Would that be the commitment to spend a year in Kinmarty, or were there other promises made?"

She felt heat rising into her cheeks.

"No. No other promises. He's my cousin's friend, not mine."

"I think that you are not being entirely honest, Ann. I think that you love him, and that he cares for you as well."

The memory of that kiss, the feelings it stirred, swamped her. Some men could steal kisses as easily as shaking one's hand. It didn't mean anything to them. She made herself shrug. "He doesn't. And if I do, I shall recover." The marquess's booming voice came through the closed door and Ann shuddered again. "Not by going meekly to the altar with someone else, though."

"You would like to choose your own husband? How very modern."

The drollness of the comment made Ann smile. "I just need to choose someone who respects me and returns my affections."

"Oh, in our world, it's never as simple as that." Her brows scrunched together, the two fine lines there deepening, and Ann remembered Urjit lifting her over the patch of rocky ground. That was truly a deep divide to jump over.

The gap between her and Errol was nothing, if the stubborn man would just forgive her for helping him.

"I don't know what to do anymore," she said. "I'm tired of being pushed and pulled. If he lives, my father will make it impossible for me to stay here and live here on my own."

"Have you the funds for that?"

"For a simple life, yes. I have some money that my father cannot touch. If that should run out, I can seek employment. Would you help me, Mrs. MacDonal?

Not financially, of course, but help me find a cottage where I can live in peace?"

Mrs. MacDonal's slim hands enfolded hers. "I most certainly will."

OVER THE NEXT COUPLE OF DAYS, ERROL SAW TO HIS three patients each morning, visited Mounth Tower and then went on to the surgery where a stream of locals appeared with various ailments. He worked late, taking his dinner at the inn before returning to the castle. The duke had servants at the ready to fetch him, should the duchess go into labor, but the babe seemed to be taking his or her sweet time about leaving the womb.

It was just as well, he supposed. The stonemason had carved the name *Robillard* into his mother's tombstone. Each day that he visited, he felt less sure about leaving Darleton to the whims of a stranger.

And Ann, it seemed, had disappeared. He hadn't seen her anywhere; not at the castle, nor the village, nor had she stopped at the surgery. They had unfinished business, but how he was to finish it, he had no idea. He'd kissed her like a lovestruck fool, and then she'd thrown her act of charity into his face. As much as she'd wounded his pride, the memory of her pliant body under his haunted his every free moment, particularly when he was in his bed.

The senior partner had written, asking him his plans. Well, he somehow had to deal with Darleton, and he couldn't leave until the duke's child was born, so that gave him some time to think.

The day after that last kiss and Strachney's accident, Errol had reluctantly escorted Rolly and Maggie to their cottage. A regular at the inn remembered Gillespie had a cousin in Glasgow, and the general belief was he must have gone there. At any rate, no one had seen him lurking about. Busby had seen to repairs on their cottage and provisions of fuel and food.

Nights had turned bitterly cold, and a few inches of snow had fallen. Christmas was but days away.

Meanwhile, Strachney's wrath had only deepened. On the third day of his convalescence, Errol found the man sitting up in bed, having just finished the beef tea and toast Errol had ordered.

"It's starving I am. I need some real food."

Appetite was a sign of healing. The man's color was also better. Errol placed a hand to his forehead. "No fever that I can discern. It appears you've been very lucky, Strachney, though it's still early days." He called over the footman on duty and told him to fetch a full breakfast for the patient.

"Very lucky," he grumbled. "Where is my daughter?"

Ann hadn't come round to check on her father? That seemed out of character. But after the abuse he'd heaped on her the day of the accident, no one could blame her for staying away. He certainly wouldn't.

"Why should she visit you after the way you spoke to her?"

"You've driven her away. Soured her on her own father. You tell her that I want to speak with her."

"If I see her, I will convey the message. Now let's have a look at this wound."

Ignoring the grumbling, he silently inspected and redressed the wound, noting it was healing nicely. Strachney would live, the beastly man, which meant he would soon resume bullying Ann to become Lady Hottentot.

"Oww."

Errol drew in a breath. "Lie still."

"You've rough hands for a surgeon."

He gritted his teeth, silently finishing the new dressing.

"Why didn't you let me die, hmm, Robillard? You might have done so and snatched up my daughter before I can change the will."

He stowed his instruments, struggling to tamp down his anger. "I'm a physician—"

"You're naught but a bonecutter—"

"A physician and surgeon, and I'd never let a patient die if I could help him. Not even such a one as you."

"Yes, well, and should you have second thoughts, if I die, Ann won't get any money until she's five-and-twenty; won't get it at all unless the trustee approves her choice of a husband. My solicitor will keep an eye on her. Wouldn't trust those fool cousins of hers."

"That's too bad. Her cousins care a great deal for her."

And so do I. And what could he do about that? Since her father's return from India, she'd lived like a princess. Like the titled lady the man hoped to make her. All he could offer her here were the keys to a broken-down tower and an estate needing to be restored on the slimmest of budgets, while he tended the sick for a pittance. If she came with him to London, she'd share humble rooms with him, while he worked long hours to improve their lot. She'd be friendless and alone in a big city. There'd be no garden for her herbs, no still room for her concoctions.

She deserved more. She deserved a life of ease.

The footman knocked and entered with a laden tray. Like a dog slavering in a knacker's-yard, Strachney licked his lips. "Bring that here now," he said.

Errol slipped out, and went to check on his other patient, the duchess. She was in her private sitting room, stretched on a chaise. Mrs. MacDonal sat next to her, a book open on her lap.

The duchess said she was tired, and irritated, and the same backache that had plagued her for weeks still bothered her, but she begged off from a closer examination and sent him off to the village.

As a groom led his mount out, another horseman trotted up.

"Dr. Robillard," he called.

It was Will, the groom who'd come to get him when Strachney was injured.

"Sir," he said, staying mounted, "that fellow Gillespie's been seen in t' village."

"Where?"

"Passin' through."

Errol swore. Gillespie would be heading home to his cottage. "Come with me, Will," he said.

Will tipped his cap. "There's more, sir. Miss

Strachney headed out that way in a gig with a basket of food. Offered to go with her, and she wouldn't have it."

Will didn't have to explain what *that way* meant. The lad and his mother would be in danger, and Ann, dear Ann.

Errol prodded his horse and took off down the lane.

"I MISS ME DA." ROLLY PICKED AT THE TARTAN COVERING his legs, his lower lip quivering.

"You love him," Ann said.

"Aye. He's not allus beatin' on us. 'Tis t' drink makes him wild."

She rose from her stool and stirred the fire. Her father didn't beat her, yet she knew what it was like to still love someone who didn't treat his own child kindly.

"And worryin'," he said, words too wise for a small child. Maggie must have told him that.

And why shouldn't Gillespie be worried? The last baron was a negligent recluse. The current one wanted to shirk his duties, to... to hand them off to someone else.

While she busied herself bringing the fortifying broth sent by Cook to a boil, her own insides roiled, despair warring with a building anger. Why couldn't these people be helped? Why wouldn't Errol help them?

She wrestled her composure back into place and picked up the battered dipper. She'd begged off from gathering more greenery with Edme, Cottingwith, and Penelope for a chance to leave the castle altogether and avoid the smug, ingratiating marquess. The last few days, one servant or another had stuck to her like glue when Edme or Penelope were otherwise occupied. Perhaps she ought to have let Will accompany her today, but she couldn't keep disrupting the work of the Castle's servants. The marquess had still been abed when she'd left, and he'd never soil his hands visiting a crofter's cottage.

Maggie had gone off to tend their chickens and see to their few sheep while Ann unpacked the food basket and watched over Rolly.

The door flew open with a bang.

"Da," Rolly whimpered, and seemed to curl into himself.

THE BARON DECIDES

*G*illespie wobbled in the doorway and the reek of whisky filled the whole of the cottage's one room.

"You," Gillespie shouted. "Ye meddlin' busybody."

Maggie appeared silently behind him, wide-eyed, her face drained of color except where the bruises had gone to yellow and green.

"I'm heating broth," Ann said. "Do you want some?"

"We don't need yer damned charity."

Maggie opened her mouth, but with a quick shake of her head, Ann silenced her. Maggie disappeared.

To grab a shovel, Ann hoped. It was too far to the tower to run for help.

"No. I see that you don't need charity. I see that you had enough coins to pour whisky into your gullet while your wife and son went hungry."

"Why you—"

"You beat your wife and broke your lad's leg. *For shame.*"

He glowered, his lip curling into a feral snarl.

She plunged the dipper into the boiling broth. "Come no closer." Rage coursed through her veins and stiffened her hands around the dipper handle. His drunkenness be damned. She wouldn't make excuses or wheedle this bully. "Rolly loves you," she said. "God knows why, the way you treat him and his mother. Hiding in your cups and only coming out to beat on the people God gave you to care for. What a lesson of manhood you're giving your son."

"Oot," he shouted and lunged. "Oot of me house, ye —" He yowled.

The dash of boiling liquid had struck square in his broad, ruddy face. While he pawed at his eyes, Ann grabbed for the poker.

"I'll kill ye," he bellowed. His fist flew. Ann ducked, raised the poker, and froze. Gillespie's next punch had jerked backward. A figure in black locked on the bully's arm and wrenched it around.

Errol. Errol was here. She glanced at Rolly. He'd raised up on one elbow, his eyes as wide as his mother's had been earlier.

Ann crouched next to the lad, her weapon ready.

Errol had his opponent on height, but the crofter was built like a barrel with powerful shoulders. He was drunk though, and clumsy.

Gillespie swung. Errol ducked and delivered a slap. "That's for Maggie." He struck again, this time harder. "And that's for Rolly. And this..." He dispensed a bone-cracking blow that had blood spurting from Gillespie's beak of a nose. "Is for Ann. How dare you insult her for helping your family."

"*Damn ye*, ye broke my nose. Who are ye to interfere here?" He leered at Ann. "Ann, is't? Aye... she's yer strump—"

Errol's fist came up under Gillespie's chin, knocking him into the wall and shutting him up.

Maggie pushed through the door, with Will behind her and Busby crowding in behind him.

"Ye fool," Maggie said. "He's the doctor as tended our Rolly's leg that ye broke."

Gillespie rubbed his jaw and swiped at a flow of blood. "Pah. He'sh nought ta me."

Errol dusted his hands. "And there's where you're wrong, Gillespie. I'm your new laird. I'm the new Baron of Darleton, and this is *my* land and *my* cottage. You live here under *my* sufferance and the terms of the lease."

Ann's heart leaped into her throat and tears welled. Did Errol mean to stay?

"Are you all right, Ann?" Errol asked, his look heated. No doubt, a lecture was coming.

She nodded, her throat too clogged to speak. So grateful she was that she hadn't had to fight Gillespie on her own, she couldn't blame him for wanting to scold her.

"Busby, Will, tie this fellow and put him on my horse. Lock him up somewhere in Mounth Tower. Tomorrow or the day after, when he's sober, I'll decide on his punishment."

Bloody spittle landed near Errol's boots. "Ye broke my nose, ye bloody—"

Errol thrust out a hand and wrenched the beak straight. Gillespie screamed.

Lips twitching, Will pulled out a length of rope and tied the bully's hands behind his back.

ERROL REACHED ANN IN TWO STEPS. HE PRIED THE POKER from her hand, tossed it aside, and gathered her into his arms, pressing her head to his shoulder. The foolish lass ought to have taken a groom with her on this mission. Gillespie would have beaten her, he was that drunk.

"Mam," Rolly said in a small voice, "will they hang da?"

Maggie went to him and shushed him. Ann looked up at Errol, eyes shining with tears.

"No, Rolly," Errol said. "I'll not see him hang."

"He loves his da," Ann whispered. "But the beatings and bullyings are not—"

"I know. What about you?" He cradled her jaw in his palm. "Will ye marry me, even without your father's blessing? Without your dowry?"

She blinked and gazed at him, wide-eyed.

"The only title I can offer is baroness, and the only home a moldy tower needing a roof and—"

She pressed her lips briefly to his. "Yes," she said.

His heart soared, and he pulled her closer, tucked his arm around her, and kissed her. Her hands circled his neck, and he lifted her higher, lips still locked, teasing her with his tongue till her lips opened for him and welcomed him in. His hand strayed down her side to the curve of her hip…

"Miss," Maggie cried. "Laird."

Laird. His mouth stilled. That was him.

"Cover your eyes, Rolly," Maggie said.

Errol pulled back and looked at his bride-to-be. More beautiful than ever she was with her eyes starry, her cheeks pink, and her lips plump from kissing.

"Oh," she said, looking back at Maggie, and blushing furiously.

"Maggie, Robby, you're the first to know: Ann has agreed to marry me."

Maggie grinned. Robby's mouth dropped open.

"Ye'll stay here then, Ann?" Robby asked. "Ye won't marry that marquess?"

"How did you know—"

"'T' whole village knows," Maggie said. "He and that other fella was runnin' their mouths at the tap last night 'bout fixin' his gamblin' debts. Talkin' aboot snatchin' ye up. Complainin' aboot the duke's servants."

Fire sparked in her eyes. "That cad." A look crossed her face. "Edme has a dowry." She tried to pull away, but he held her.

"Cottingwith will protect her. We'll send a note to the duke, but he must already know how blatant the scheming's become. He's no fool."

"Oh, Errol."

She collapsed against him again and his heart filled, the fierce tenderness overwhelming him. He held her like that until her trembling subsided, and then set her back.

"Come up to the tower with me," he said. "Have you ever visited there?"

"No. Your grandfather wouldn't admit me."

"It's a wreck. Might give you second thoughts."

"I don't care… or… I've been such a fool. It's true, I love it here, but I love you more. I'll go where you go." She cupped his cheek. "And plain Mrs. Robillard will suit me. We'll go to London. Only…" She glanced back at the boy and then whispered, "please, don't let my father have Darleton."

He thought of the practice in London. A great opportunity it was, yet perhaps it would be there after he sorted matters here. And if not, well, with Ann by his side, he was at peace with whatever was to be.

"I rather like the idea of being a baron," he teased.

"A doctor baron," she said.

"With a wife making potions in the still room."

He gave her a long look. They'd marry this very day over the anvil, or in this case in the great hall at Mounth Tower. Busby and the servants could witness. But first…

"Let me just check that Rolly's leg is mending." He touched his lips to hers and stepped around her.

The lad's forehead was cool. The wound on his leg was healing nicely. The break—time would tell how well he'd set it. "You'll stay off this leg a while longer, you hear," Errol said. "Let the bone heal."

Rolly wrinkled his nose, but Maggie grabbed his hand and kissed it. "Thankee, laird. Ye saved us."

147

Embarrassed, he mumbled his farewell and led Ann out.

A light powdery snow was falling, and the gig crawled down the rocky lane to Mounth Tower. Errol needed all his attention to keep from veering off into a ditch.

Ann was unaccountably quiet.

"Having those second thoughts?" he asked.

She shook her head. "I'm only wondering if you've forgiven me for helping you with the school fees."

Help from a woman—his wife. What would people say? He decided he didn't care. "I must have."

The gig tipped and righted itself, and he concentrated on the road for the rest of the journey.

ANN SENT UP A SILENT THANKS WHEN THEY PULLED UP to the door at Mounth Tower. Will and a wizened groom ran out and led the horse and gig off, and Errol escorted Ann to the front step and the open front door.

On her only visit to Mounth Tower, this was as far as she'd made it. The butler—the same elderly man who'd sent her away—stood at attention. Lined up behind him were two footmen, two housemaids, and a scarecrow of a woman who must be the housekeeper. None of them were younger than sixty.

How *did* they manage the heavy work?

Busby pushed to the front. "Baron, I've seen to that other matter. May I introduce your house staff? Please come in out of the cold."

Ann held back. This was Errol's grand homecoming, not hers. Not yet. Or so she thought.

Her feet left the ground and she found herself in his arms, clutching his shoulder, and laughing as he set her feet down on the slate tiles. "You must meet your new baroness also, the former Miss Strachney."

"We're not married yet," she whispered.

"No? Ah. We need more than Maggie as a witness."

He smiled down at her, sending heat into her cheeks.

The servants openly studied Errol, and she saw curiosity in their faces. The women's gowns and aprons, though clean, were old and had been mended in places. The men's livery gleamed from wear, and their wigs sported bare patches.

"Is there a decent bed in this house with clean sheets?" Errol asked.

"Ye mean to stay the night?" the housekeeper asked.

The butler sent her a silencing look, which didn't stop the bold woman.

"We'll ready two chambers for ye," she said.

"One chamber," Errol said, a questioning gaze fixed on Ann. "If you'll marry me now, Ann," he whispered.

Her heart pounded fiercely, remembering the kisses they'd shared. If they married now there'd be more than kisses, this very day, a lifetime of them. A shiver went through her.

He wrapped an arm around her. "Light a fire in the great hall and gather around."

Footsteps scurried around her and she leaned into Errol's warmth. His eyes twinkled down at her.

"Marrying now," she said, smiling back at him, "will be fine."

ERROL HELD HER WITH ONE HAND AND LIFTED A CANDLE with the other as they followed the elderly butler's candle up the creaky staircase. It was otherwise too dark to see your hand in front of your face.

Which perhaps, thought Ann, was better, since she was suddenly feeling nervous. She had no more than her shift to sleep in, and this on a night so bitterly cold.

At the door of the chamber, Errol dismissed the servant. She watched his candle bob down the stairs, anticipation and anxiety rising in equal parts.

The latch turned, the door opened, and blessed warmth greeted her, along with light from the fire and a dozen beeswax candles lit about the room. The table held a covered dish and a bottle of wine. Such extravagance for so poor a household.

"Oh, I can't eat a bite more," said Ann. After their brief wedding in front of their witnesses, the factor and servants of Mounth Tower and Will, who'd stayed for the wedding before dashing back to the castle with Errol's quick note to the duke, they'd been served a surprisingly good meal—plain fare, but good. She was touched by the kindness of Errol's servants.

Her servants, too, now.

"You'll want to eat later." He lifted her cloak away and went to work on her lacings.

His fingers brushed her skin as he worked, sending ripples of awareness through her, and she could feel his warm breath and—oh. His lips touched her neck, even while his hands continued to move down the back of her gown, slipping it open, pushing it over her shoulders and down until it fell at her feet.

The stays came next, and then he was lifting her up and out of the pool of clothing and carrying her to the big bed. Fingers shaking, he untied a garter and slowly, slowly rolled down the stocking and tossed it aside. Then his fingers traced a path up the same leg, paused at her nether regions, making her gasp, and moved on to the other garter and stocking.

She lay back on her elbows and watched as he tore off his coats. His shirt flew away revealing a muscled chest, and desire licked into blazing flames.

He unbuttoned his fall, grinning down at her. She felt the challenge in that grin and sat up, defiantly staring while her body throbbed with that same something she'd felt when Errol was kissing her.

"You're going to make me blush," he teased.

He turned away and it felt like a victory until he pushed his trousers down and she saw a well-muscled bum.

She fell back with a giggle and covered her eyes.

In seconds, he stretched beside her and took her into his arms. His hand crept down her leg and then back up again, taking the hem of her shift with it.

"I wish I had a better nightgown for this night," she said, all nerves again.

"Another time," Errol said, kissing her. "I'd be delighted to have you in my bed wearing nothing at all. Might even prefer it."

A gasp escaped her. His hand had found its way to her nether regions again. She sat up suddenly, tore the shift over her head, and turned fully to him.

The look in his eyes dissolved any trace of her nerves.

THE FIRE HAD DIED BACK WHEN AN URGENT KNOCKING woke Errol. He rubbed his eyes and disentangled from his beautiful wife.

"What is it?" she said, stirring.

"Shhh. Go back to sleep."

He found his trousers and donned them, then pulled his shirt over his head.

"Beg pardon, laird." It was the butler, still in his nightclothes with a robe thrown over. "Message from the castle." He handed over a missive. "Her grace is in need of you. Sent over two horses and begs that Mrs. Robillard attend also."

Errol scanned the brief note. Her ladyship's water had broken at four in the morning. "We'll be down in a trice."

As soon as the door closed, Ann pushed back the covers and searched out her shift. "The babe is coming."

"Yes. We are both summoned. Here." He tossed over her gown. "I'll lace you as soon as you're ready."

Two of the Kinmarty grooms had come to provide escort, the snow having fallen all through the evening and night. Local men, they knew the way, and they led them through the difficult drifts of snow. Still, it seemed to take forever, and the sky was beginning to lighten when they reached the castle.

Clutching the bag he'd carried, Errol hustled Ann in.

THEY PASSED TWO FOOTMEN STATIONED IN THE corridor and found the duchess in bed, the duke seated beside her. A maid hovered nearby.

"It's about time, Robillard," the duke said.

"Shush, Andrew." The duchess managed a wan smile. "Dr. Robillard came as soon as possible." Her smile broadened as Ann took her hand. "And Mrs. Robillard. I'm so happy for both of you."

"I'm sorry we were delayed, duchess," Errol said. "How is the pain?"

"Wrenching," the duke said. "You must do something for her."

"I fear the hard labor will be yours, duchess," Errol said, "but I'll do all I can to help you."

"We both will," Ann said.

Errol went to the basin, sleeves hastily rolled, and scrubbed. He nodded to the maid, who handed him a towel. "Bring in more water and some fresh linens."

What else would he need? He'd assisted with many births, but never a duke's child. *Heaven help him.*

Ann caught his eye and the faint smile she sent calmed him. She was here, contained and composed.

While the duke fretted, Ann slipped to the side of the bed and held the lady through a contraction. He glanced at the mantel clock, made a mental note, and returned to the bedside.

"Fil, love." The duke gripped her shoulders. "Good God, Robillard. *Do* something."

Ann murmured a soothing sound.

"This is all in accord with the natural process, duke," Errol said.

Lips pursed, the duchess eased in a breath. She didn't appear to be a screamer, but perhaps she was sparing her husband.

He needed to examine her soon, but the duke's presence made things more awkward.

"I'm staying right here," the duke said.

Errol sent Ann what he hoped was a meaningful look.

The duke stroked his wife's cheek. "Are you cold?"

"I'm fine, Andrew. Well, not entirely fine."

Ann signaled and a maid, a different one, brought over a cup. "Have a wee sip of the caudle, and then let Errol examine you." Ann held a cup to the duchess's lips and glanced at him. "I had the kitchen prepare it. It's only a weak wine posset."

He nodded and watched her assist the duchess, with the same gentleness she'd shown the lad, Rolly.

When Ann moved back, Errol leaned over the bed and began his assessment, checking for fever, unearthing an arm and wrist to count the beats of the duchess's pulse. Though the room was warm from a blazing fire, a heavy blanket was pulled up to her bosom.

He stepped back, deciding how to go on. From past

examinations, it appeared the presentation was not breech, but he'd like to palpate the lady's abdomen again, and measure her cervical opening.

Preferably without the duke being present.

Errol checked the clock again. Several minutes had passed. He doubted birth was imminent. And if it wasn't, it would be helpful for the duchess to walk around the room a bit or at least change her position.

The duke whispered endearments and fussed more with the blanket, pulling it up to his wife's chin. Errol and Ann exchanged a look.

Another contraction made the duchess gasp, quietly, her face showing her agony. Ann crawled up onto the bed on one side and held her, while the duke supported her other side.

Sweating and panting, the lady fell back, and the duke, his face ashen cried "Oh, my darling, Fil."

"Duke," Ann said firmly, "You must promise not to faint. And you mustn't interfere with Dr. Robillard. He needs to do more than check for a fever or a racing pulse. He needs to look at her... her opening and see if it's time to push, or if she must labor longer. Isn't that right, Errol?"

"She's right," the duchess croaked. "Andrew, do move out of Dr. Robillard's way."

Ann rose and came around to touch the duke's arm, leaning close and whispering something.

He leaned over his duchess, told her he loved her, and bestowed a kiss on her forehead.

The tender scene sent a bead of sweat trickling down the back of Errol's neck.

When he glanced at Ann, she sent him a shiny-eyed smile, and his confidence lifted.

"I'll be nearby," the duke said.

"Don't worry," Errol said. "All will be well," he added, praying that was true.

He glanced back and saw Ann escorting the duke out.

AN ARRIVAL, A FISTFIGHT, AND A
BITTERSWEET FAREWELL

*H*ours later, Errol exchanged grins with Ann and handed her the squalling newborn.

Outside, the light was growing to a fine Christmas eve afternoon, snow brightening the landscape. As he delivered the afterbirth and tended to the exhausted mother, he could hear Ann murmuring as she cleaned the bairn.

Edme entered with an armful of linens. Another maid followed with more hot water. Ann held the swaddled child for the women to see.

"Is all well?" the duchess croaked.

"Perfect," Ann called. "We'll let Dr. Robillard have a closer look, to reassure the duke." She was as radiant as the painting of the Madonna at St. Mary's in Edinburgh. He shook off his need to touch her and reached for the babe.

Their hands brushed as she passed him the

newborn, and color rose in her already rosy cheeks. Her eyes filled with… a poet might call it wonder.

She was beautiful. Their wedding night had been glorious. In fact, he could hardly wait to get her back to whatever room the duke would allow them, because there was no going back to Mounth Tower in this snow. And her help with the birth had been a godsend, her composure easing his one or two worries.

She smiled and went to assist Edme and the housekeeper with changing the linens and freshening the duchess. He turned away and opened the loose swaddling. The shock of cool air roused an outraged wail.

"Well, doctor?" the duchess called.

"Healthy lungs," he said. "Ten fingers and ten toes, and all the rest of the apparatus looks to be in good working order." He rearranged the swaddle.

The door opened a crack, and the duke poked his head in.

"One moment," Ann handed Edme a brush. "Tidy her hair." She caught Errol's eye, beamed him a smile, and hurried to the door.

The new father needed *his* hair tidied and his neckcloth retied. One glance, though, at his smiling wife at least restored his color.

"Dr. Robillard," the duchess called, in a surprisingly strong voice, "let the duke hold his son."

Mrs. MacDonal swept in then with fresh caudle, and a servant arrived with a tray of food.

Ann came to stand by him. "I'm so happy for them," she said.

"As am I." He took in a breath. The scene unfolding sent his insides tumbling and the need to be alone with Ann was almost overwhelming.

Errol rolled down his sleeves and donned his coat, nodding to Mrs. MacDonal.

"He'll be hungry soon enough." The duchess had proclaimed she would nurse him herself. "Put him to the breast as soon as he fusses. If there's a problem, call me."

"I've nursed me own five bairns," the housekeeper said. "Don't ye fret, doctor. I'll show her grace just what to do."

"Well then. I'll return anon. Let her sleep if she wishes. Ann, my love…" He pulled her aside and swept her into a kiss.

"Enough of that," the duke called. "Go and announce your marriage at luncheon."

Errol pulled her along into the corridor. "I must see your father first and tell him our news myself."

"I'd like to go with you."

"Then so be it."

They traversed the corridors until they found the room where Strachney had been recuperating. Pausing outside the door, they heard voices.

"I tell you, it's not possible," Strachney said.

"No?"

That voice belonged to the marquess.

"It's all the buzz of the stables."

"I'll take a horsewhip to—"

Ann slammed the door open before he could stop her.

"To whom, Father? To me? Or to my husband, Dr. Robillard, Baron of Darleton?"

The marquess' angry gaze moved from Ann to Strachney and back again. "So, it's true."

"Aye," Errol said stepping forward. "And you, Hottentot, your wager in the public house with your friend, Warton, what you said about snatching up Ann to fix your gambling debts, is all the buzz of the stables and the village. And for that…" He planted a facer on the arrogant prick.

"Why you…" Hatherot lunged, and Errol dodged him.

"Do you deny it?" Errol asked.

The marquess slid a glance to Strachney, who had sat up, his lip jutting out. "Of course, I do."

A MELEE ENSUED, AND ANN OPENED THE DOOR TO CALL for help, but found two footmen and a maid already standing by. The men rushed in; Ann sent the maid to fetch more aid.

Hatherot was no dandified nobleman or drunken crofter, and he landed a punch that would have broken Errol's nose had he not moved away in time. Errol was no delicate flower either, but a braw man who'd dealt with drunks in his father's inn and the hard men who worked the warehouse and docks.

She'd seen fights like this between the Beecham boys when they were younger, and once or twice on the street. She stood back, biting her nails.

Errol landed a staggering punch that knocked Hatherot back into the wall.

"I say, Robillard." The marquess rubbed at his jaw. "If doctoring doesn't work out, you could make an excellent living in the ring."

Errol's fists came up. Ann ran and pulled him back. "Thank you for defending my honor," she said.

"Honor?" Strachney waved a hand. "Ye rattlebrained girl. What did ye expect? A marquess wanting to marry so low, and a plain girl to boot. Dammit. Pigheaded, headstrong... ye ought t' have obeyed. I'd have negotiated a proper settlement; ye'd have the title without him getting all my money. Now ye won't have anything from me, nor a title except a paltry Scottish barony. My daughter, married to a black innkeeper's filthy brat."

"That's quite enough, Strachney." The duke stepped near the bed. Lord Cottingwith hovered in the doorway behind Edme.

"Pah." Strachney threw back the covers. "Fetch my clothing," he told the footman. "And have the stables ready my coach. I'm leaving."

She glanced out the window. The snow was still falling. "You're the pigheaded one, father," she said. "It's been snowing all night and all morning."

"I won't stay another night here."

With a nod from the duke, the footman departed.

"Perhaps, Hatherot, you'd like to depart with Strachney and enjoy the hospitality of Glenthistle?"

Hatherot's hand paused on the jaw he'd been rubbing. He smirked. "Gad, no. Don't mind a mushroom, you know, but this fellow…" He dropped his hand and bowed to Ann and Errol. "I beg your pardon, Miss Strachney… er Mrs. Robillard, I suppose you are now. And Dr. Robillard. All's fair in love and war, eh? Good fight. If you're ever in London and want to go a round or two, look me up."

He bustled his way to the door, and suddenly turned. "The heir's arrived safely, duke?"

The duke escorted the marquess out, discussing his son, quickly turning the conversation to his plans for hunting.

Ann hurried to the dressing table and fetched a towel. Tears blurred her vision as she dabbed at a cut on his face. "No one's ever fought for me before."

He tossed the towel away, pulled her into his arms, and kissed her. She tasted blood and pulled away. "Your lip… and your eye, and… Sit down and let me check what other injuries you have."

"*Get out of my bedchamber,*" Father roared.

"Not here, my love," he said, grinning. "Is your room nearby?"

A giggle pierced her consciousness. Edme covered her mouth. The earl was biting down trying to hide a smile.

"I shared with Edme."

"Mine then."

Her heart filled and stretched and started to overflow. She cast a look back at her father. She'd waited so many years for his return from India, prepared to love him. Maybe someday she would.

"Goodbye, Father," she said.

EPILOGUE

*A*nn closed the bedchamber door softly and settled the lantern on the scratched and faded wood of the bedside table. The room was blessedly warm, Forbes having arranged for a couple of the older servants to tend to the cottage while Ann and Errol attended Kinmarty's grand Hogmanay celebration.

Not long after midnight they'd trudged home through the fresh fallen snow. This year's cèilidh, and the more refined party for local gentry in the great hall, had been far more subdued than the one the year before. All the Kinmarty guests had left: her father, Warton, the marquess. Even Cottingwith had been unexpectedly called away.

And even Edme. Though Edme denied any tendre for the earl, Ann knew her cousin. Edme's hopes for a romance of her own had been dashed, so Mrs. MacDonal had escorted her home to Edinburgh.

In the short few days since their hasty marriage,

Errol and Busby had laid out a plan for the Darleton estate and its tenants. Improvements for the crofters would come first. In the meantime, she and Errol would reside in the snug, warm, convenient rooms of the doctor's surgery.

Hurrying out of her gown and stays, she slid a flat box from under the bed and opened it. Peeling back the layers of tissue paper, she lifted the filmy white silk and lace gown and spread it gently on the counterpane. It was, Mrs. MacDonal assured her, new and never worn. She'd bought two of them as gifts for the duchess, but, she'd added slyly, a hastily married bride would need it more.

For Ann, it was another wish fulfilled. She hoped Errol would like this New Year's present.

The silk felt cool against her skin, and she moved close to the fire, raking her fingers through her loose hair.

"Ann." The muffled growl came from behind the closed door and sent shivers up her spine.

"Come in," she called, her voice shaking.

Errol stepped in, his gaze moving over her, a slow grin forming. With shaking hands, she picked up the decanter and splashed whisky into two glasses. "A toast to the new year?"

Errol took the glass and slid his other hand around her waist. His gaze moved again and hovered on her lace covered breasts.

"Here's to you, my love," she whispered, clinking her glass against his, and taking a sip. The whisky heated a path through her, making her shiver.

"My love," he murmured. He drained his drink, took hers in the same hand, and set them both aside.

"Well?" she asked.

One large finger traced along the lace edge of the gown's bodice, and then back again, lifting a strand of hair at her neck. Ann swallowed a gasp, waiting, but Errol said nothing.

"Do you like it? I l-longed to come to you in a proper nightgown."

"It's beautiful," he said. "You're beautiful. And I love you." He pressed his lips to her, the kiss gentle and brief. "Shall I tell you what I longed for? A proper honeymoon. A chance to lie abed with my bride and make love to her the whole day through."

She thought about the frantic week since their rushed nuptials, the heartbreak of the break with her father, and Edme's sad farewell.

"Sweet Ann, have I frightened you?"

She smiled up at him. "Not so far."

He threw back his head and laughed. "I'll let you sleep a bit," he teased. "I promise, I'll do my very best to make you happy, now and forever."

"Oh Errol." She pressed her hand to his strong jaw. "Life can be bittersweet, but I *am* happy. Whatever troubles arise—"

"We'll face them together."

He swept her up into a kiss and then pulled away. "After our proper honeymoon."

The End

If you enjoyed Ann and Errol's story, please consider leaving a review on Goodreads, Bookbub, or the bookseller's website of your choice.

A NOTE FROM THE AUTHOR

I hope you've enjoyed revisiting Castle Kinmarty, the setting for the first book in this series, *The Duke She Despised*.

In researching this story, I learned that higher education could put a considerable dent in a family budget, just as it does now. Regarding the privilege of fishing on private land, eight thousand pounds seems like a great deal of money, but I found that tidbit of information in a travel diary of the period.

Many thanks go to my writer friends at the Bluestocking Belles, Caroline Warfield, Jude Knight, Sherry Ewing, Rue Allyn, Elizabeth Ellen Carter, and Cerise Deland for their encouragement in finishing this book, and especially to Jude, who edited the final manuscript. Thanks go also to Dar Albert of Wicked Smart Designs, who created all the beautiful covers for this series.

In case you're wondering, Edme's story is in this works. Look for it to arrive in autumn 2023.

To find out more about my books, visit my website, https://alinakfield.com, and sign up for my monthly newsletter.

All the best,

Alina K. Field

ALSO BY ALINA K. FIELD

Sons of the Spy Lord Series

Marrying Mr. Gibson

Previously titled *The Bastard's Iberian Bride*

Paulette Heardwyn rushes to visit her dying guardian, set on learning the truth about her father. But the only man with answers takes his secrets to the grave, leaving her penniless— unless she marries his illegitimate son

The Viscount's Seduction

Lady Sirena Hollister has lost everything, even her fey abilities. But when the fairies hand her a chance at a London Season, her schemes for revenge stir up an unknown enemy, and spark danger of a different sort, in the person of a handsome Viscount.

The Rogue's Last Scandal

Falling—literally—into the arms of the *ton*'s most outrageous rogue seems a risky path of escape, but Maria Graciela Kingsley y Romero has no other choice. Only England's greatest spy lord can help her, and he is not to be found—so his son will have to do!

The Counterfeit Lady

Vowing she'll never submit to an arranged marriage, an earl's daughter bolts for the seaside cottage that will someday be hers. But she finds her quiet refuge occupied by the last man she ever wants to see—an American artist, who's also a thief. And, quite possibly one of her father's spies.

Avenging the Earl's Lady

The long war is over, but honor requires vanquishing one last enemy, and the Earl of Shaldon has no time for romance. But when the lady he longs for interferes in his plot, and his enemy strikes at her, nothing else matters but avenging his lady.

Novellas and Holiday Stories

The Marquess and the Midwife

A Christmas Novella

Finalist, 2016 National Reader's Choice Award

Uncovering a lie drives a new marquess back from a self-imposed exile at Christmas to find the only woman he's ever loved. Finding her turns out to be easy, uncovering her stunning secrets, a bit harder. But winning her back will be the greatest challenge of all.

A Leap Into Love

A Sweet Regence Romance Novella, a sequel to

The Marquess and the Midwife

Can a gentleman be too charming?

The ladies of Upper Upton think so.

When the single ladies of the village conspire to teach their charmer a lesson that might bankrupt him, the town's loveliest young widow—who's sworn off marriage forever—steps up to warn him.

Liliana's Letter

Finalist, 2015 National Reader's Choice Award

The Matchmaker Meets the Matchbreaker

Liliana Ashford's future as a professional chaperone depends on her wealthy charge's successful marriage, but her own close encounter with a scoundrel years ago makes her determined to save the girl from the same kind of rogue.

The Ghost of Depford Hall

A short, sweet Halloween story, a sequel to

Liliana's Letter

It's her mother's last All Hallows' Eve.

When family, friends, and tenants gather, goblins, ghouls, and ghosts are banned from this All Hallows' Eve party.

Only, no one told the Ghost of Depford Hall!

Courted by the Earl

Previously titled *Bella's Band*

A 2015 RONE Award Finalist

Saddled with his brother's title and debts, nothing about this new life makes the Earl of Hackwell want to stay—until he meets a lady with a secret that can change everything.

Rosalyn's Ring

2014 Book Buyer's Best Winner, Novella Category

Done with grieving her losses, a late nobleman's daughter has fallen into a tidy spinster's life in London. But when one snowy Christmas Eve, a young woman needs rescue, she seizes the chance to do good—and to recover a family heirloom that ought to be hers.

Haunting Miss Fenwick

Thrilled to finally have a permanent home, a Squire's daughter won't let a supernatural creature scare her away. While hunting the ghost she doesn't believe in, she stumbles upon a mysterious flesh and blood man who might be the key to all of her problems.

The Upstart Christmas Brides Series

The Duke She Despised

Hiding her true identity, a young vicar's widow takes a position as housekeeper in a remote Scottish castle at Christmas for a new duke who years ago sabotaged her chance for happiness. She quickly falls for the duke's charming but not very competent factor, not knowing that he's hiding something also—he's the duke she despised!

Convincing the Countess

When a business-minded aristocrat encounters a fetching widow he knew years earlier as the bride of a ne'er-do-well earl, temptation steers him along a track that may derail all his plans. Can he convince her to set a course for her future that includes him?

The Impetuous Heiress

Before dashing Lord Loughton can make amends with his neglected fiancée, the lady's meddling cousin delivers her to his doorstep. He soon realizes more is amiss than his carelessness. Can he uncover her secrets and win her back before he loses her altogether?

The Macbeth Series

Fated Hearts,

A Love After All Retelling of the Scottish Play

A Scottish Baron returning from two decades at war meets the wife he divorced and the daughter he disavowed before she was born, only to learn that everything he'd believed was a lie. Determined to win back the only woman he's ever loved he must first face the viper who drove them apart.

The Comtesse of Midnight

A Scottish Earl on a quest for the elusive Comtesse de Fontenay, rescues a French lady smuggler during a devastating storm, taking shelter with her. As the stormy night drags on, he suspects she knows the lady he's seeking, the lady who holds the secret to his identity.

Claims of the Heart

Since a perilous fall, Lucie Macbeth has been seeing more than a settled future as the heiress to a Scottish barony. The visions plaguing her include a man—one far above her class and breeding, and English to boot. He's engaged to a duke's granddaughter as well, and thus wholly inappropriate. Though she can't marry him, and she won't become any man's leman, when the Sight warns her of danger to him her conscience, and her heart tell her she can't walk away.

Find out more at https://AlinaKField.com

and sign up for my monthly emails for news about upcoming books and sales.